THE PERILOUS ROAD TO HIM

BOOK THREE OF THE ROAD SERIES

N. L. BLANDFORD

ISBN 978-1-7776601-9-2 (Paperback Edition)

ISBN 978-1-7781341-1-1 (EPUB Edition)

ISBN 978-1-7781341-0-4 (Kindle Edition)

Some characters and events in this book are fictitious. Any similarity to real persons, living or dead, is coincidental and not intended by the author.

Published by: Natasha Backs

Permission to use material from other works:

Front cover image by Shutterstock - andreiuc88

Author photograph by PhotoHuch

Visit nlblandford.com

To Candice and Megan.

PROLOGUE

STRANGER

People no longer notice when they're being watched. The hairs on the back of people's necks used to tickle and stand tall when unknown eyes focused on them for more than a few seconds. Now, the hand-held screens absorb their attention and mute the sense of danger. Even when I sit right beside them.

Being a part of the Hammond family taught me how vital observation skills are. The difference between life and death lies in one's surroundings.

I thwarted attempts on Helen Hammond's, the head of the Hammond family, life when fingers twitched at a man's side like a cowboy in preparation for a duel in the center of an old dusty western town. Or drops of liquid death glistened under the light of the crystal chandelier before falling into Helen's glass. Attempt after attempt was stopped because I watched. Everyone.

Yet, it was all for nothing. When it counted most, I failed.

For years, I watched Charlotte and saw nothing more than another loyal maid. Her actions and her demeanor did not alert me to the danger she would cause. I hate myself for being fooled by her.

Charlotte is the reason Helen is dead.

She and Olivia Beaumont.

The first time I set my eyes on Olivia, I knew she would be trouble. Visitors to Hammond Manor are in awe of the estate and the world around them. Olivia was morose and scrutinized everything. The smile plastered on her face was forced.

Helen also held concerns with the unannounced visitor, but her loyalty to her nephew, William, hindered her from handling the situation. She said William was the future of the Hammonds. To go after Olivia, if we were wrong, would have created a divide in the family. Helen wanted evidence Olivia did not belong in the family. The other obstacle was the possibility William had turned against her and knowingly brought a threat into the family. If so, Helen would need to eliminate them both. A task she could not take lightly. Understandable; however, I believe when a family is as powerful as the Hammonds; you take no risk of waiting and do what needs to be done and you move on. The family would have survived without William succeeding Helen. We could have found someone just as smart, calculated, and ruthless.

We could have brought Helen's own son out of hiding.

Helen's shame and fear of reprisal from within her own ranks meant any acknowledgment he existed was minimal. Almost obsolete. Having a son with someone other than her husband would have been a disgrace; an embarrassing example of her lack of self-control. If Helen raised the boy, she would have lost the respect of those within her father's kingdom. Therefore, Helen found another way for the family to survive, should she die, and ignored her son.

I did not. I prepared him for what I hoped would be his return to the family. His adoptive parents and I made sure he knew where he'd come from and the heights he could climb. We taught him the essential skills to be a successful Hammond. Observation. How to run illegal businesses alongside legal ones. Coercion. Deception.

Prior to Olivia's arrival, Helen silenced me anytime I brought up her son. However, once Olivia's true identity came to light, combined with Charlotte's deception and desertion, the concrete walls of the empire cracked. We both knew if we didn't do something, the foundation would collapse.

Helen listened, but through conversation after conversation, she wouldn't agree to bring her son home. When she finally conceded, it was too late.

MI5 was like a pack of lions waiting for their prey to be at their most vulnerable before they pounced. Introducing Helen's son into the equation would have killed all future hope for the family. MI5 would have learned of him and monitored him for the rest of his life.

Our secret weapon was best kept hidden.

Helen's son was so well hidden that even Olivia didn't know he'd been a part of her life for eighteen years.

CHAPTER ONE

CALVIN

A throbbing pain in the back of my head awakens me. My heart wants to jump out of my chest. The tips of my fingers are numb from the cold. I crack twigs and crush leaves under the weight of my body as I push myself up to a seated position. The dark forest spins around me. I squeeze my eyes shut to stop the nausea. The sea salt in the air sits on my tongue. My fingers find a large bump protruding from the back of my head. I recoil from the surge of pain the simple touch causes. I don't feel blood, but I look at my hand. Then I look at the other one.

My heart stops and my breath gets caught in my throat. Even in the rays of the moonlight that seep through the dense summer canopy of trees, there is no mistaking that the palms of my hands are red. Dark red. The backs of my hands are not as dark, but are a faded red just the same.

Drops and smears of red and brown paint my sweater. My jeans are too dark to reveal what stains may live on them. One of my shoes is missing, the other stained like the rest of me.

My breath returns in a large gulp, and my hands shake. How did I end up here? What happened?

I look around and scream. Leaves scatter while I crab walk away from the body of my friend, Shaylynn, and back myself up against the trunk of a large tree. Shaylynn's face has frozen in a state of terror. Her yellow sweater and white jeans are the home of pools of blood.

I gather my courage, crawl towards her, and whisper, "Shaylynn?"

No answer. Her chest is unmoving and her open eyes point towards heaven.

I take her wrist, a faint warmth kisses my hand. I try to find a pulse. She can't be dead. Please God, she can't be dead.

Nothing.

She needs help. No one else is here, only shadows of darkness.

I place her hand back beside her body. Tears burn my eyes. I push away the hair glued to Shaylynn's face. Even in death, she is beautiful.

All sense of time lost, I sit staring at her. I'm numb and confused. What happened to my friend? How am I covered in blood? Is it Shaylynn's? I would never hurt the one person in this world who understands me. Right?

Flashes of Shaylynn running away from me flood my mind. Her face looks as scared as it does now. Why had she been fleeing from me? Was she afraid I'd hurt her? My head throbs, trying to recall what happened.

Leaves rustle in the distance. I look around but can't see anyone. If I hurt Shaylynn, then I need to get out of here. I don't want to leave her behind, but I don't want to be found beside her either.

Branches fight back as I run through them. I grip whatever I can as I struggle up the hill and out of the forest. With each step, sharp stones and twigs pierce my shoe-less foot. I ignore the pain until I break through the forest's edge and stop under a street lamp. Leaning over my knees, I try to catch my breath.

Everything around me takes on a rough blur. It's like I am looking through a very narrow telescope and can only see what is in front of me. Blobs of colour speckle my peripheral vision. Houses. Cars. A post box. I hobble down the street. Pain erupts through my foot and up my leg. I pull out a pine needle from my shoe-less foot. The tip of the needle has blood on it.

My adrenaline dissipates, and exhaustion takes over. My limbs feel heavy. More scenes from this evening replay in my mind. Shaylynn and I walking along the boardwalk, our hands holding ice cream cones. Chocolate for her and Black Cherry for me. Shaylynn's eyes are full of excitement. She takes my hand and smiles.

A hand on my shoulder startles me and pulls me from the memory.

I swing around and my shoulder bashes into someone. I look down and find Mrs. Olson on the sidewalk.

"Sorry to startle you, Calvin, but..." Her eyes trace my body from top to bottom. Her eyes widen and her jaw hangs low. Mrs. Olson pushes herself away from my outstretched hand until she can go no further and leans against the stone wall in front of her house.

I want to apologize for knocking her over, but all I can say is, "I'm not my father."

Chapter Two

Olivia

The alarm clock on my bedside table flips from 1:33 A.M. to 1:34 A.M. The blue hue of the numbers torments me. Night after night, perspiration travels down my spine, and pools at the bottom of my lower back, while I lie awake and watch the minutes, followed by hours, descend into the next morning. Waiting for Calvin to come home.

If my concern for Calvin didn't keep me awake, my nightmares about William would. It's been eighteen years since I watched him die in a ditch. His life was taken by my gun. After all this time, he still has me trapped. Trapped so deep within myself, I find it hard to trust anyone. Not completely. I barely trust myself to keep everything together for Calvin.

I hug the quilt I made after Calvin and I first arrived in Woodhaven. The edges are worn from trailing behind Calvin everywhere he went as a toddler, and from my worried rubbing now as I wait for the front door to creak open.

Once a month, Charlotte begs me to talk to a therapist, but I can't. I'm worried they are eyes for the Hammonds. For William. I fear whatever weakness I show will make its way back to those who survived the Hammond's demise. They will then find Calvin and I, and they will kill us. To keep us safe, I need to keep my past to myself. I don't even risk telling Calvin who I was before we came to Woodhaven.

Besides Charlotte, the only other person privy to this information is Reverend John Buckley. Even then, I hadn't intended to reveal my secret. He only found out because the weight of it became too much and he rushed me to the hospital halfway through one of his sermons. My memory of that day has sketched itself in my brain.

I'm seated in the uncomfortable wooden pew at the back of a two hundred-year-old church. The sun casts colourful rays through the stained glass windows and paints the stone floors and the church's occupants. I'm only half listening to the Reverend preach about being truthful to oneself, and those around you, when my chest becomes tight, like cinder blocks sit upon it. Air becomes difficult to swallow and I heave as I grip the back of the pew in front of me. My nails dig into the wood. I pull myself to my feet, looking to escape the confines of the crowd. The church.

In the aisle I trip over myself. My arms catch me before my face smacks against the stone floor. Reverend John stops speaking and the eyes of the crowd focus on me. Anxiety's winning the fight. My arms are too weak to pick myself up and my tears disobey my wishes and release themselves like a waterfall. My heart beats so fast it hurts.

The birthmarks in both of John's eyes are the last things I see before my world goes black. H's is the first face I see when I wake up, even as my eardrums are hit with beeps from machines & rain pelting the hospital room window.

John's years of service to the community have equipped him to recognize a panic attack. For me, he doesn't drop the subject of finding its source. Was it out of frustration, or exhaustion from holding onto a devastating past for so long, that I open the vault to my past?

The moment I unleash my demons, I feel lighter. I'm also scared. Lying in that hospital bed, I knew very little about the man I shared my secrets with. Before I moved to Woodhaven, Charlotte completed background checks on the town's residents. As far as we knew, there was nothing to worry about with John.

However, my mind dances in circles. What if the checks missed something? What would happen if my fears about being found by whoever remained in the Hammond network came true? I retreat back into my shell and avoid John for months after my panic attack. I revert inward so much that Calvin's meals are inedible. Charlotte's Aunt Maud is the only reason my son is still alive. Time and time again, she keeps my life together while I'm falling apart.

John comes by the house every day. Every day, I turn him away. Until one weekend when Charlotte, Aunt Maud, and five-year-old Calvin force me to get dressed and join them for a nice Sunday roast dinner. Calvin is excited we are having a party. It's the excitement in his eyes that makes me agree. No one told me that John would also join us.

I put my best face on, for Calvin, and make it through the meal. The heaviness of the memory of that fateful day in the church grows with every minute. John spots the invisible emergency flares going off around me and invites me to go for a walk with him. I refuse, but Aunt Maud corrals me into my jacket, and out the door, like a parent wrangling a child into a snowsuit for school. Annoyed and uncomfortable with the situation, I find myself chilled by the spring breeze dancing off Woodhaven Bay as John and I stroll along the cliffs.

John's the first to speak. "Full disclosure. Charlotte's been keeping me apprised of how you've been doing."

"Lovely. Now I have two babysitters. I'll need to have a talk with her about that. What's happening in my life is not her news to share."

"She's worried about you. I also think having someone else sharing the burden it takes to carry the secrets you both have stowed away helps her."

"Great, well, the two of you are more than welcome to talk about her past, but I'd appreciate it if you'd leave mine out of it."

"I understand why you are apprehensive about trusting me. I've been where you are. Someone I trusted betrayed me after I shared information I had asked to be kept secret. I must have confessed a thousand secrets to my mentor, confidant, and friend; however, it only took one revelation of a secret to destroy that relationship. With it, a small seed of doubt and distrust rooted in my head with every secret I've shared with someone thereafter."

"Just because morphine loosened my lips, doesn't mean I trust you, or that I want to trust you. You talk about knowing how it feels to be betrayed and therefore won't betray me, but how am I supposed to believe you?"

"That answer has to come from within yourself, but why don't I share the secret that changed my life? Would that help?"

"It's a start." I was going to get something out of this forced encounter. A secret was as good as anything else this time could bring.

"What I'm going to share may have shattered my life, but the damage it caused does not compare to what you have been through." John pauses and runs his hands through his dark hair. "I was out with some friends when, one drunken night, I had an affair. I regretted my actions the moment the tryst was over. For two weeks, I'd been trying to work through how to tell my fiancée, when I came home one evening to find all of her stuff gone. No note. No answer when I called. My friend, who unbeknownst to me, had been in love with my fiancée, seized the opportunity to wedge a knife between her and I. They ran off together."

"Wow. What a shitty friend. If she ran away with him, I'd be asking other questions, but that's not the point of your story."

"I've had those questions. Especially, as they were married three months later and are still together. I've lived in Woodhaven ever since. Right where God wants me to be. I know it's not the same, and even if you don't believe it, you can trust me. I don't want to cause you the same pain I had. Whatever you tell me stays between us."

"And Charlotte."

"You were the one who informed her of what you told me. I have revealed nothing. When she talks to me, I try to guide her based on her own experiences. It helps her to heal, knowing she doesn't have to hold back when we talk."

"Well, I'm glad she's getting something out of her conversations with you. Can I go home?"

"You're going to keep ending up in the hospital if you bottle up your past. How close were you at dinner to having another severe panic attack? I don't mean to sound preachy, but think about Calvin."

"How dare you-"

"Listen, I'm not trying to tell you how to parent your child. I'm just saying, ever since you moved to town, you've carried this secret. The longer you try to do that alone, the harder it's going to become."

"I have Charlotte."

"And look what's happening to her. She buries herself in her work, day and night. She no longer visits, all to avoid the darkness that surrounds you. I'm sorry if my words hurt, but you aren't happy and you make the people surrounding you unhappy."

"Thanks for the pep talk."

"What I'm trying to say is, let me help you carry your burden. I'm not someone to fear. If I was, do you think Charlotte would trust me?"

He has a point. Charlotte is the Director of of Special Operations - Human Trafficking at MI5. It's her job to question everything and everyone. Maybe I'm being paranoid and can't see a friend when he stands right in front of me.

"Fine, but I'll only talk to you so that I can be a better mother to Calvin. Not because I trust you. If I get any sense that your intentions are not honourable, I'm walking away. From you and this town."

"Deal."

Hours pass as we walk up and down the cliffs, cementing our footsteps into the grass. Calvin is in bed when I get home and Charlotte has caught the last train back to London. For the first time, I go to bed without fear. Perhaps I'll get my first full night of sleep without the aid of alcohol.

For one night, I have a reprieve from the deep, torturous voice of William. The next night, and every night after, his voice returns in the moment right before sleep is about to take me over.

As I wait for Calvin, William visits me earlier than normal. His voice taunts me, "You deserve nothing but revenge for Adam!" followed by, "I love you. This was all for you. I was going to do my time. Then we could be a family."

William's face morphs into a younger version of himself. The shared steel-blue eyes, prominent nose and sharp chin reflect a nightmare I want to forget, but relive every day in the face of our son. My son.

The voice of a fear I try to keep buried in the back of my mind gets louder. *Calvin's becoming him. There's nothing you can do about it. It's in his DNA. The icy stare, sharp tongue and violent temper. You can't deny it any longer. Calvin is William.*

I bury my face in my pillow and scream. Why do I hide it? I'm the only one home. One more scream and I long to sleep.

I take a deep breath and say a prayer. I need help to separate Calvin from William. I pray for Calvin's safety and for him to come home.

Ever since Calvin's sixteenth birthday, he's been distant. Not just towards me, but his teachers, coach and mates. He's doing just enough to graduate his final year of school in July, but any slip-up could jeopardize it. He picks fights with players on his football team when they make an error on a play. Unprovoked, he snaps and becomes unrecognizable to me. He throws whatever's in reach at me during his fits of rage. A toaster almost fractured my arm.

My bedside clock turns to 1:43 A.M.

For two years, I've tried everything I can think of to find my son. The one who told me silly jokes every morning to start my day with a smile. The one whose attempts at making me breakfast in bed resulted in smoke alarms and food explosions in the kitchen. Now, I receive barely audible responses, if I get any at all.

I keep telling myself he's a teenager. This is normal. Even if I don't like it. I think about what caused such a dramatic shift in Calvin's personality. Nothing stands out. It's as if one day he was here and the next, he turned sixteen and someone had flipped a switch. The son who returned home that night fueled the fear I had given birth to another William.

1:45 A.M.

Gravel rumbles in the distance. Bright white light fills my room and disappears after brakes screech to a stop below my bedroom window. A car door slams.

All the hairs on my arms stand on end. I reassure myself it's just Calvin announcing his arrival home. Nothing to worry about. I roll onto my side, face my bedroom door, and wait for the hallway light to turn on.

KNOCK, KNOCK, KNOCK.

The door's unlocked. Even drunk, Calvin would know that. The static buzz of the doorbell starts and doesn't stop. I'll rip the finger off whoever's standing outside.

I wrap myself in the blue housecoat from the foot of the bed and hover my hand over the nightstand. I leave my gun. Whoever was at the bottom of my narrow stairs may deserve to be shot, but if they meant to hurt me they wouldn't ring the bell. "Hang on, I'm coming. Jesus fucking Christ, give me a minute."

I open the door and regret my choice of words. John stands before me. "Oh shit, sorry about the whole Jesus Christ thing." My ears echo the buzz of the now silent doorbell.

"When have you ever changed how you speak around me?" John gives me a weak smile.

He must have dressed in a hurry as his short dark hair is a mess, pieces sticking in every direction. He isn't wearing his typical black shirt and white collar, rather a tattered Ramone's t-shirt and blue jeans.

John's eyes focus on me without blinking. The small dark birthmarks inside his eyes reflect the full moon. He keeps biting his lip. "Can I come in?"

"What's wrong?" I step aside. The smell of a sweaty sleep trails John.

"I think it's best if we talk in here."

John always waits to be invited to sit, however he's already seated on the couch when I enter the living room. Goosebumps sprout on my arms. Whatever is going on surpasses a small, worrisome act of defiance by Calvin.

Weary of what John wants to tell me, I brace against the arm of the couch and lower myself beside him. John sits up straight, shoulders wide, but he has a hard time meeting my eyes. I ask the universe to not be told that Calvin's dead.

"Has Calvin done something? Is he alright?" I've done everything I can to protect him. From the world. From my past. If something has happened to him, I will never forgive myself.

"Calvin's fine. Physically speaking."

"Well, what other kind of speaking is there?"

"I don't know how to say this. Which is odd, given my job and all. You'd think-"

"John, stop stalling. What happened? Just rip the Goddamn band-aid off." There's no apologizing.

He unlocks my gripped hands and holds them in his. "Calvin's in custody at the police station."

"What? Why?" My stomach eats my heart.

"They found him covered in blood."

"I don't understand. Whose blood?"

"The police aren't aware yet, but it wasn't Calvin's. He has no injuries that would generate that much blood."

"How do you know all of this?"

"DI Whitaker called. Calvin asked to see me."

"You? Why wouldn't he call me? His own mother!" I pull my hands out of John's grasp and push myself up off the couch. "Wait. You've already seen Calvin? Why didn't you come get me right away? Why are you only here now?"

"I had suspected Calvin was drunk, and that the police were trying to scare him by bringing him to the station. I just thought it would be a conversation and a ride home. Nothing to worry you over."

"Nothing to worry me over. Have you often driven Calvin home drunk? You know what? We can talk about that later. I need to see my son." John grabs my wrist and tries to pull me back down beside him, but I refuse to move. I need to leave the room, but John's strength keeps me where I stand.

"I'll take you to the police station. But first, I need to tell you something else."

"Tell me in the car." I wrench my hand free.

"Calvin was talking about his father."

My knees buckle and I fall back onto the couch. Calvin doesn't know about William. However, he has no reason to be talking about the father I'd made up for him. Not at two o'clock in the morning. Especially not at the police station. "What was he saying?"

"He kept repeating 'I'm not my father.' I couldn't get him to talk about anything else."

My shoulders drop forward and I clench my chest to comfort the pain that wields itself inside. Calvin's mutterings could only refer to one person.

William Hammond is once again back from the grave.

CHAPTER THREE

CALVIN

The hard plastic and metal chair is unpleasant and I keep shifting my position to get comfortable. A chill travels through my cheap blue sweater and sweatpants. I'm too scared to look at the two-way mirror to see the state I'm in.

I'm brought into the police station, placed into a cell and ordered to stand on top of a large white sheet of paper. They make me undress and put all of my clothes into brown bags. Even my underwear. Why would they want my underwear? One officer brushes my hair and with each yank of the hairbrush, the paper below me crinkles. Once they have scraped under my fingernails, I step off the paper, disturbing none of the leaves, dirt, and other particles I can't see, but suspect are there.

Now, I'm in a closed interrogation room. The hard plastic and metal chair is unpleasant and I keep shifting my position to get comfortable. A chill travels through my cheap blue sweater and sweatpants. I'm too scared to look at the two-way mirror to see the state I'm in. I stare at the door and wait for someone to walk into this eerily quiet, dull room. A small string tied to the air vent shaft whips back and forth.

Reverend John came and saw me, but he didn't stay long. He's probably gone to get Mom. She's going to be so mad. Let her be. It's her fault all of this is happening.

The lock on the interrogation room door clicks and a man wearing a cheap brown suit enters. The only distinctive feature about him is his one brown eye and one blue eye. On a normal day I would find that more intriguing. Right now, I'm focused on getting out of here.

With the man, is a woman dressed in a dark police uniform with her cap under her arm. I recognize them both from around town, but can't recall their names. The man may have spoken at an Anti-drug, or some nonsense, assembly at my school. An assembly where I would have paid more attention to Shaylynn than to the speakers.

The man takes a seat across from me and a loud buzz emits from the machine on the table. He states the date and names the people in the room: Sergeant Sarah Cole, Detective Inspector Daniel Whittaker, and Calvin Lyons.

"Calvin, I have to tell you that as you are eighteen, I am able to interview you without a parent, guardian or lawyer present. I gave you the leeway of calling Reverend John; however, he is no longer here. You do not have to answer my questions, however, you're a good kid and whatever happened tonight must've been a misunderstanding. So why don't you tell us what happened?" He taps his pen against a small black notebook. Each whack reverberates in my ears.

I pick at my cuticles, and they bleed. I've been trying to remember what happened, but I can't put the pieces together. I only see bits and pieces from before we step into the forest. She was teasing me about the supposed ghosts that haunt Woodhaven Bay and Woodhaven forest.

"Calvin? Are you listening?" DI Whitaker's voice pierces my thoughts.

"What? Sorry. I don't remember what happened."

"What do you mean, you don't remember? They found you covered in blood, Calvin. Someone doesn't just forget how that happens."

I shrug my shoulders. "I'm sorry, but I-"

"You've gotten into a lot of fights lately at school. A real temper on you, I hear. Did someone make you angry and you lost your temper?"

Why won't they say Shaylynn's name? The image of her pale body floats in front of me. Fingers snap.

"Calvin! Pay attention. Whose blood is all over your clothes? Are they hurt and need help? Calvin, you can help them if you tell us. Do you want to help them?"

I nod. My mouth tastes like cotton balls. "I-"

The metal door swings open, and my mother rushes towards me. An unimpressed officer comes in after her, takes in the scene and addressed DI Whitaker, "sorry about that sir, she got past me and I-"

"Enough. We'll handle it."

The officer exits and the bustling from outside the interrogation room disappears once the door is closed.

Mom's dressed in the worn T-shirt and sweatpants she sleeps in. Her arms wrap around my head. Her chest feels warm and I can feel her rapid heartbeat. She kisses my forehead before she crouches down beside me. Her swollen eyes search mine for answers.

"Are you okay?" Mom asks.

I nod. The sadness evaporates from her eyes as she turns on DI Whittaker. "Are you questioning my son without me present?"

"He's an adult. There's no requirement for you, or anyone else, to be here."

Mom looks like her head will explode. "Well...Well, I need to speak with him. And in a room where no one can watch us." She looks at the mirror.

"We'll make sure no one is on the other side."

"I'd rather go somewhere else."

"Unless you want to discuss your unauthorized entry into the secure area of a police station, you'll remain here." DI Whitaker nods to Officer Cole who stops the recording. An unspoken stand off takes place between my mother and the DI before she and I are left alone.

"Calvin, I need you to listen to me. You cannot, under any circumstances, talk to the police until I find you a lawyer. Do you understand?"

"Yes," I mumble.

"Good." She runs her fingers through her hair, there's sadness in her eyes, but it's different. One I've never seen. She's been sad and angry most of my life, but not like this.

"Mom? I'm scared."

She sits beside me and rests her hand on my leg. "I know. We'll figure this all out, okay? Together. Like we always do. I doubt they'll give us much time, so I need you to tell me everything that happened. I promise I won't get angry. Just help me understand so that I can help you."

"I don't remember."

"What do you mean, you don't remember?"

"Shaylynn and I spent the night at the fair by the pier. We walked along the boardwalk and then headed into the forest. But that's where I stop remembering. Then I wake up and she's dead." The dam of tears closed off from my tear ducts break free. The wall of water can't hide how pale Mom's face has become. She takes me in her arms. They do nothing to comfort me. My best friend is dead and I might have killed her.

A knock on the glass door causes us to part. Her hands rest on my arms. Sergeant Cole pops her head in. "Sorry, but you'll have to wrap this up soon."

My mother's head falls and she musters a small smile for the officer. After the door closes, she holds my head in her hands.

"Here's what's going to happen. DI Whittaker is going to come in here and I'll tell him you will not speak to him until you have a lawyer. They might still try to ask you questions, but I suspect they'll give us until tomorrow. Pretend to show that they are cooperating. A show of good faith, they'll call it. They will keep you in a cell here until they can speak with you."

"Can't I come home with you?" I've never longed for the comfort of those walls more than I do at this moment.

"I wish you could, but when someone is...killed, they won't let anyone they suspect might be involved go home right away."

"But they don't know about Shaylynn."

"What do you mean?"

"I don't think they've found her yet. They kept asking me whose blood was on my clothes and never mentioned her."

Mom bites her lip and brushes the hair from my forehead. "Right, I'm not a lawyer, but if John's account of where they found you is accurate, they'll find her soon. If I was Shaylynn's parents I would be worried about why she hasn't come home. You said you two were in the forest. Is that where she is?"

"Yes."

"I'll tell DI Whitaker about her. You say nothing. Understand? There's something else you need to know." Mom presses her soft lips against my forehead and holds them there for a few moments. "Given the seriousness of the situation, the police are within their rights to hold you for up to twenty-four hours. They could also apply to the courts to have that extended to ninety-six hours before they have to release you or charge you with a crime. If I can't get you released, then you will be remanded to a prison. You'll likely have to stay there until a trial is done."

"But I...How do you know all of this?" I'm aware of how. But would she tell me?

"From Aunt Charlotte."

Lie.

"Look, we can talk more about that later, but I wanted you to be prepared for what might happen. We need to work together to make sure you can come home, okay? I'll find you the best lawyer I can, but is there anything else you can tell me? What about how you found her?"

Do I have to keep repeating myself? What more did she want from me? "I told you I don't remember! It wasn't me. Right?"

Mom's hesitation lasts milliseconds, but it speaks volumes. She's always careful when I get angry, as if I was a ticking time bomb and one misstep would cause me to explode. Tonight, she's right. My blood boils and I toss Mom back and throw my chair. It catches the side of the black metal tape recorder. Both fall to the floor and neither registers a dent to mark the event.

"You think I did it?" Mom shrinks away from me. "You've never trusted me. Not once. Well, if I did this, it's because of you! Not because of some DNA you fear. Not because William Hammond is my father."

Frozen in place, her wide eyes stare into the abyss while officers, reacting to the commotion, pull me out of the room. I kick and twist for freedom as they drag me towards the cells.

"It's your fault!"

CHAPTER FOUR

OLIVIA

I try hard to keep myself together in front of others. I hide my tears and fears from the outside world. Calvin's words shatter my armor. To hear those words come out of his mouth, words I prayed I would never hear, break every piece of me. 'Father. William Hammond'. Words more powerful than any weapon.

I'm heavier than I was when I entered the room, and struggle to stand. Officer Cole tries to help me off the worn-out tile, but I swat her away. She stares at me for a moment and leaves.

I need to think. After everything I've done to protect my son, he blames me for what's happening to him. Is he wrong?

I had every intention of telling Calvin who his real father was. About the evilness that seeped out of every pore of William. I hoped if he understood where he came from, he could avoid turning into the same monster. But every time I gathered up the courage, Calvin's smiling face made me waver. I didn't want to extinguish his happiness, and I told myself I would tell him tomorrow. And then the next day. Tomorrow turned into eighteen years.

Keeping the secret became easier than telling him. I didn't want to ignite the inevitable anger that would come with telling him something he should have known sooner. Or worse, risk unleashing whatever evil might live deep inside my son. I didn't want to lose my sweet boy.

Now, look at him. The miniature William I feared I'd given birth to has surfaced.

The glass door swings open and John pulls a chair towards me and hands me some water. "Are you okay?"

"Am I okay? What sort of question is that?"

"I meant-"

"They found my son covered in blood. Shaylynn is dead. He's blaming me for everything and he knows..." I gulp down the water but am wishing it's something stronger.

"Shaylynn's dead? Lord have mercy. Have her parents been told?"

"No. The police don't even know yet. But I'll tell them. I need a minute to compose myself first."

"You said Calvin knows something?"

"About his father."

"Which one?"

"William. I wish it was the one I made up."

John sits back in his chair. His shoulders slump forward. "Oh. I take it you weren't the one who told him?"

"No."

"Then who?"

"I'm not sure, but I don't want to talk about this here. After I speak with DI Whitaker, can you please take me home?"

"Of course."

The hinges on the interrogation room door squeak to announce our exit. I want to leave the secrets exposed in the room behind, but that won't help Calvin. I find DI Whitaker huddled with other officers on the far side of the room. My feet propel me toward a man who now controls Calvin's future. My future.

"DI Whitaker juts out his chin and releases a heavy sigh. "I'm not releasing Calvin."

"I don't expect you to."

"Then why are you here?" Not an ounce of kindness sits on those words.

"You're looking for Shaylynn Taylor in the forest. Calvin isn't sure of the precise location," I struggle to release the next words, "she's dead."

With little reaction, DI Whitaker takes out his phone and updates the search party, his eyes locked on me the entire time. He kicks at a torn edge of the carpet and continues. "Start around Mrs Olson's. If he made it to her house, I doubt the body can be too far from there. Work your way out in all directions. No one leaves until you find the body." DI Whitaker's phone returns to his jacket pocket. "Did Calvin say anything else?"

"I want to help here. I would hate to be Shaylynn's parents. However, Calvin can't remember what happened."

"And you believe him?"

"Yes." DI Whitaker didn't need to know I was asking myself the same question. "I'll let you get back to work, but no one is to speak with Calvin alone. I understand you have a job to do. But mine is to protect my son and ensure he does not become a technicality of the legal system."

DI Whitaker raises an eyebrow but keeps silent.

"Unless there is anything else, I'm going home."

"We'll need to search your house."

"Get a warrant and you can toss everything in it. Otherwise, no one steps inside."

"You wouldn't try to tamper with evidence, now would you, Ms. Lyons?"

What would I do to protect my son?

"I assure you that both of us want to find the truth and give Shaylynn's family answers." Without waiting for DI Whitaker to speak, I dash out of the police station. John trails behind. I'm so focused on figuring out how I will get Calvin out of jail, and who may have told him about William, that I don't notice the person in the brown trench coat. My shoulder collides hard with the stranger. The collar stands tall and masks most of their face. We both apologize and go our separate ways.

The drive home, on the curved seaside roads, is short, but it gives me more than enough time to run through the handful of people who were aware of William.

My best friend, Charlotte. Eighteen years ago, she used her connections, after a farce of a trial, to arrange a rendezvous with William during transport to his permanent prison. They sentenced William to less than the minimum time required, a measly thirteen years for human trafficking and money laundering! The benefits of paying off the judge. Murder should have been another charge against William, but there was no concrete evidence to tie him to the dead bodies found on the Hammond Manor Estate, one of which was buried there because of a direct order William gave the person who pulled the trigger.

When the judicial system failed, Charlotte decided we would take the law into our own hands. In a ditch, on the side of an empty road, my bullets ensured my eyes would never lay upon the body of William Hammond again.

Charlotte had full knowledge of William. However, she respects me enough to say nothing to Calvin, or anyone, without my permission.

Next, there's Charlotte's aunt, Maud. She took Calvin and I in when we first got to Woodhaven. She became a mother to me. However, as far as she was aware, my past involved a terrible relationship with a violent man. Not which one. I don't know why, but I could never bring myself to tell her. I wanted a fresh start and didn't want her, or anyone else's, pity.

Then there was John.

CHAPTER FIVE

STRANGER

Classical music sings from the gramophone in the corner. Open a crack, the mahogany doors for the speaker below the turntable emit a low volume of music. I would prefer to allow the full soothing sounds of the strings and piano to escape the machine; however, at this late hour, my neighbours would not.

Red, orange and yellow embers dance in the fireplace as blocks of ice circle my whiskey glass. Every step I took over the last eighteen years has led me to tonight. I will savour this moment, but only for tonight. There's a lot of work left to do and I will not get distracted from my path.

Olivia Beaumont's house of cards is about to collapse, and I need to make sure the pieces fall where I want them to. I need her to feel what I felt as Hammond Manor faded into darkness in my rear-view mirror. Loss. Betrayal. Guilt. I'll never walk those halls or hear Helen's voice again. I should have spoken louder, pushed harder, to get rid of Olivia. It's my fault the Hammond empire shattered, and we all became outcasts in the criminal underworld. It's my fault Helen and William are dead.

The day Olivia killed William, hatred enveloped me. I almost killed her on the train. One trip to the bathroom and she would have struggled to breathe, her heart seizing as an untraceable drug ate the life out of her from within. My grip on the syringe gave me life. It also gave me an idea.

Why rush to kill Olivia? The worry she carried on her face would torment her for months. Years. It was better to wait until Olivia no longer looked over her shoulder. Once she was happy, revenge would be more satisfying. She laid in wait in Los Angeles and at Hammond Manor. I would lie in wait and strike when I could do the most damage.

It's taken years of putting all the pieces into place and now my time has come to avenge the Hammonds. To avenge Helen and feed off the darkness from Olivia's destruction. Her distraught face in front of the police station tonight was only the beginning. I will litter the path to destruction with torment.

The record has run its course and I slip it back into its cardboard sleeve. I pull out a Glenn Miller record and place it on the green velvet turntable. The needle kisses the groove and the notes filter into the sitting room air. A calmness comes over me.

I pull back the curtain hung along the inner wall of the room, stand back and sip my whiskey. The sweet caramel flavour rolls along my tongue. I look over all the work I've completed to get to this moment. People used to call a smaller version of this type of thing a vision board. I call it a revenge wall.

There are only a few spots where the dark blue and gold wallpaper hint at its existence below news articles, photos and my own notes. Years of planning. Helen's and William's dreams for a momentous future ended because of information stored on a computer. I will not make that same mistake.

The glossy photos are smooth to the touch. Moments captured of Olivia and Calvin's life in Woodhaven over the years. A progression of Calvin's growth into a young man is documented. The eyes, sharp jawline and the waves in his hair are a remarkable reflection to a man Helen hailed as the future of the Hammond empire. Flashes of William cross Calvin's face while he and Olivia eat ice cream at the beach or fight over cereal in the food mart. From afar, I caught each twitch of Olivia's mouth and eruption of unnecessary anger while she saw William grow up in front of her.

No matter how hard Olivia tries, or how much she drinks, she can't bring herself to see Calvin as himself and not his father. I feed off this fear.

My finger stops on the faded registry document for Olivia's driver's license. The last name Beaumont erased from existence and Lyons written in its place. However, a name change is only an illusion of comfort. I'll give Olivia credit. She's kept her past hidden from the gossiping residents of Woodhaven. Although Aunt Maud and Charlotte helped. Aunt Maud put the town in its place when people started asking questions about the latest arrival in their sanctuary. Everyone believed Olivia was escaping an abusive relationship and needed to protect herself and her son from the wrath of a monster. Charlotte's MI5 access, and ability, erased most of Olivia's past from the prying eyes of amateur sleuths. Those who didn't know what they were looking for.

My eye catches a newspaper article of Olivia standing outside her bookstore, Word Haven, during a charity event for the local library. Every book was two to five pounds, and one pound from every sale helped fund a Children's Reading initiative. The event drew the entire town, and people from neighbouring ones, in droves. Olivia didn't notice that Aunt Maud sold me ten books that day.

I pinned the article with hundreds of others. Olivia's life as a detective on the Toronto Police Service, back in Canada; the fire and investigation into William's work in Los Angeles, and the trials of Helen and William for money laundering and human trafficking. Full page articles as the world became enamored with the case. Yet their deaths went undocumented. A likely ploy by MI5 to avoid reporters asking questions and digging deeper into their causes of death. My grip on my whiskey glass tightens.

My eyes rest on a photo of Calvin and Shaylynn, walking the pier while seagulls fly overhead in the heat of the summer sun. It was just before Calvin turned sixteen. The smile on his face is so large one would think nothing could ever remove it.

A week later, seated across from me at a coffee shop, the smile faded into memory.

CHAPTER SIX

OLIVIA

John pulls his car up the drive of my quaint grey sandstone house, tucked away on a small hill, just outside the heart of Woodhaven. I purchased it two years after my arrival in town, at a point when I was confident there were no stragglers from the Hammond's criminal empire on the hunt for me, and we wouldn't need to run at a moment's notice.

Wilkes Cottage isn't the most luxurious place in the world. However, I'm done with luxury. Three months trapped in a mansion in Los Angeles, and then another five months at Hammond Manor here in England, was more than enough for me. The mountains of money they used to cover up the horrific treatment of their victims never made me grateful I lived like a queen. One with no power and beaten, but a queen nonetheless.

Simple, homely and quiet was what I wanted. When Mr. Wilkes passed away, his children were more than happy to offload the property. It needed a lot more work than they wanted to put in, so I got it cheap. It was the first place I've ever owned and I cherish it.

The only benefit from being forced to marry William; to keep up his charade of my identity, was the inheritance I received after I killed him. What William did to cover his tracks meant Calvin and I had money from the few legitimate Hammond business ventures, to fall back on if we ever needed to. Wanting nothing from the man who ruined my life, I try hard not to use the money. However, I needed to get Calvin out of the tiny apartment above the bookstore.

It wasn't even an apartment. It was a room Aunt Maud converted from storing inventory into a makeshift living quarters. Calvin and I shared a double bed, which also acted as our couch. The bottom shelves of a cheap bookshelf held our food, and the top two shelves held our clothes. A hotplate sitting on top of a miniature fridge acted as our stove. A high chair and a scratched up wooden chair sat around a four person circular dining table. We had to use the bookstore's bathroom, which contained the smallest shower I'd ever seen. I'm not sure what a bookstore needed a shower for, but I was happy it was there. The place meant Calvin, and I, had our own space.

Aunt Maud had offered to let us stay in her one-bedroom flat, but she had been helping so much already I didn't want to be more of a burden. After two years of updates from Charlotte that now stragglers from the Hammonds were coming after me, and no evidence to think I was in danger, I thought I had found my place in the world. There would always be a nagging feeling in my gut that there was still a danger out there, but my love for my son, and Woodhaven had quietened it. The bookstore apartment could no longer contain us.

As a result, I bought a piece of land with a rundown cottage. Months of work, and Wilkes Cottage was a respectable home. Aunt Maud, a few contractors Charlotte completed exhaustive background checks on for me, and John all helped to make the place livable. The home was more than a slight upgrade.

John's skills don't just live in the pulpit. He's a carpenter, plumber and all-around handyman. The one I call when I can't fix something, or feel the answers from the Internet are in another language. He's the one person in this town Calvin and I lean on. I don't know what I would do without him.

With the car parked, I rest my head back against the seat and look over at my friend. His dark hair, yet to be tamed, matches the colour of the bags growing under his exhausted and sad eyes. "Would you like me to come in?" John asks.

"I could use help to figure all this out. But there's one condition."

"Which is?"

"Don't go spouting stuff like 'everything happens for a reason', or 'God has a plan', et cetera. I'm aware of all this and right now, if those words cross your lips, it'll only make me punch you. I need to focus on the events of the night. Not their potential spiritual meaning."

"I can agree with that. Although, if you broke my nose, it might fix this small curve in it." He squeezes my hand and gets out of the car.

All jokes aside, if John was the one who told Calvin about William, he would get his wish. I'll talk to him about his role in the reveal of William later. Right now, I need to understand what my son did, or didn't do.

I toss my coat over the banister and run up to Calvin's room. If there are clues about what happened tonight, I need to find them before DI Whitaker gets here.

I open Calvin's bedroom door and a foul odor hits every receptor in my nose. Clothes, both clean and dirty, tossed everywhere. The primary culprit of the stench is an open gym bag sticking out of the closet. Beside it, a pizza box where the cheese of the last slice has molded over. How had a closed door trapped the smell in?

"Where can I help? And what are we looking for?" John asks from behind a hand covering his nose and mouth.

"We need to check everywhere. The bed, dresser, his desk and his closet. You take the bed. I'm not sure I want to know what might hide in and around there. Try to find anything about Shaylynn."

While John crawls over and under Calvin's unmade bed, I rummage through his closet. The desire to plug my nose is strong, but I push through. With two fingers pinched together, I pick through the gym bag. Nothing.

The shelf in his closet has boxes of childhood toys and memories, but nothing that would help me right now.

I turn to his dresser. The top holds football trophies, an array of empty deodorant containers, and colourful snack wrappers. I pull out every drawer and scrutinize them. Inside and out. Nothing. I stick my head into the body of the dresser itself. Nothing. I pull the dresser out from the wall. Nothing taped to the back. Defeated, I replace the drawers.

"I might have something." John weasels his way out from under the bed. "Here." He hands me a ratty shoe box.

It contains small handwritten notes from Shaylynn.

"Can't wait to see you after science. Mr. Tursley is such a bore."

"Great game yesterday! You looked like a professional footballer. But didn't your mother ever teach you how to tie your cleats tighter? I've never seen a pair come undone so much."

"I can't wait to get out of this town! A few more months and we can leave."

"There's nothing about William or any sign that Calvin and Shaylynn were fighting. I don't like the one about leaving town, but this is all useless." My frustration is mounting and I toss the box aside.

"Isn't it odd that the notes even exist?" John asks.

"How?"

"Aren't teenagers always on their cell phones? Why wouldn't they just text each other?"

"My guess, they wrote them during class. The one good thing about St. Mary's is there are no phones allowed in the classroom. If the teacher catches a student using a phone in class, they lose it for two weeks. Locked up in the school office. All the parents, and students, sign a letter every year that they understand and will adhere to the policy."

"I guess I slept through that school council meeting. Parents are happy to have their child without a phone during a potential emergency?"

"As you said, teenagers love their phones and wouldn't do anything to jeopardize having them. I don't think there has been a confiscation since Calvin started there. Besides, before tonight I would question what type of emergency would happen in Woodhaven that couldn't wait until someone found a neighbour. But I guess everything changes after this." I plop myself onto the desk chair and swivel to face the black screen. The login screen loads and I type in the agreed upon password, Mar23@2020. Calvin's birthday. Not the most secure password, but one we could both remember.

The password you've entered is incorrect. Hint: Friend.

Had I made a typo? Although, what does the word 'friend' have to do with Calvin's birthday? I re-entered the password.

The password you've entered is incorrect. Hint: Friend.

"What the hell? Calvin and I agreed I would know the password to his computer."

"How many teenagers want their parents going through their stuff?"

"It was part of the deal for him to keep it in his room. Now I know he's hiding something."

I type in Shaylynn. Still locked.

"I assume you tried Shaylynn?"

"Yes!" I bark. "Sorry, even with his dramatic shift in personality, I've tried to respect his privacy. Give him room to figure out who he is. It has killed me not to snoop through his things. I've stood outside that door, my hand hovering over the door handle, but I walk away. I want to be the trustworthy mother he can turn to for help or friendship."

John raises his eyebrow and looks around the room.

"This is different. This is life and death. Now, how the hell am I going to get into this fucking thing?"

"Why don't we have some tea, with an added kick, and take a moment to think about all of this? Come on, let's-" The floor creaks under John's foot. He shifts his weight back and forth. The creaks get louder with each movement. John steps back and removes the blue striped rug. "There are no nails in this floor board."

"What?" On my hands and knees, I pull up the piece of wood.

Someone stacked a treasure trove of items under the floor. A complete 360 from the life that lives above it. But it's not the organization that makes my heart stop and pushes me back against the desk drawers.

It's the note on top that reads, "You hurt me. Now I will hurt you."

CHAPTER SEVEN

CALVIN

The cream-colored cement walls are closing in around me. The thick metal door, and the two tiny slots within it, are sealed shut. All evidence of life outside my cell evaporates when the lock clicks and secures itself in place.

The lights go out and darkness is all there is. Not that there is anything to look at. Even the cold bench I sit upon is cement and built into the cell. No pillow. No blankets.

I reach out my arms and the tips of my index fingers kiss the walls on either side of me. If I can keep my arms up, perhaps the walls will stop trying to crush me.

After a while, my arms are tired. I lie down and try to force my eyes to stay open. I'm afraid of what I will appear if I close them. My heavy eyelids win the battle. Scenes project against the back of my eyelids.

Shaylynn smiles at me as we sit upon the bluff. Cut scene. A bloody knife raises in the air. Trees stand tall behind it. The knife cuts through fabric. Shaylynn screams. I pull the knife back towards me. It's painted red. Shaylynn's eyes are the biggest I've ever seen. Questions for me float inside of them.

I wake drenched in sweat. The prison jumper sticks to my skin.

Were those my hands? I was standing right in front of Shaylynn. They have to be mine. When the knife pierces...I stop the thought from forming. Maybe I don't want to know what happened?

Cold seeps into my bones. I curl up on the bench and cry. I won't ever see the smile of my best friend again. The one person in this world who makes my life better, is gone.

God, why is this happening? Why did you take Shaylynn? It should be me covered in a sheet in a morgue. Not her. She could've made this world a better place with her laugh, let alone her dreams to help the less fortunate. What am I going to contribute to this world? Nothing! Especially without her.

Grief pins me to the bench.

I need to think of something else. Anything else.

Leonard.

My father. Or so I believed.

The abusive, alcoholic member of a motorcycle gang never existed. Mom showed me a picture of a guy on some stupid social media website older people use. Years of questions I asked about my father were answered with lies or avoided altogether. I'm sure she has excuses lined up for why she hid the truth; but I don't care. I'm her son and for my entire life, she said that it was her and me. *We* had to take care of each other. No one else would be there for us. Her lies put me in this cell. I'll never forgive her for this!

I pound the side of my hand against the wall - Argh!

My real father, William Hammond, was a criminal. The stuff he did to people was horrible. From what I've been told, and found on-line, he wouldn't be a father I would want in my life. But that's not the point. The point is, had Mom told me the truth, I wouldn't have had the life I loved ripped out from under me on my sixteenth birthday.

A birthday card tucked away in my backpack with a Daily Telegraph article folded inside revealed the truth. A picture of my mother, holding me as a baby, outside a London courthouse, with an inset photo of William Hammond, in similar clothes to what I wear now. Scrawled in red pen above the article, "*Your real father*". At the bottom, "*Tell no one. Meet me at The Coffee Shed in Coltam tomorrow after school if you want to hear more.*" I reread the article until I had memorized it.

I hid it, and the card signed "Your Friend" under a loose floorboard in my room before Mom got home from work. I put anything I didn't want Mom to access there.

I spent hours going over any news article and videos I could find about William Hammond.

Dinner on the night of my birthday was quiet. No matter how much Mom tried to engage me, I just sat and stared at her. She was someone I thought I knew, but no longer recognized. Someone I'd trusted. I picked at my fried chicken. And then the cake. I wasn't hungry.

She built my entire world on lies. She'd even lied about who she really was. She didn't tell me she'd been a police officer. Or about my grandfather, who's still alive somewhere outside of Toronto. Is he aware I'm alive? Mom also never mentioned I had an Aunt Claire who had been brutally murdered. Okay, you wouldn't tell an eight-year-old the gruesome details, but you at least tell them she existed.

My life hasn't been the same since I learned the truth. My dreams of Oxford are a distant memory. I could care less about a higher education. All I want to do is run, far away from here. I don't care what I do as long as I do it with...Shaylynn. Damn it! Now that dream has been taken away and possibly by my very own hands.

The darkness that overtook me after that day with M takes a stronger hold of me. Recalling all of the lies makes my blood curdle. Because of her secrets, I turned to a stranger for answers. A stranger who cares more that I have the truth about who I really am than my own mother.

The darkness that overtook me after that day with M takes a stronger hold of me. Recalling all of the lies makes my blood curdle. Because of her secrets, I turned to a stranger for answers. A stranger who cares more that I have the truth about who I really am than my own mother.

CHAPTER EIGHT

OLIVIA

John and I both stare at the note. "You hurt me. Now I will hurt you." I reach for it. John grabs my wrist. "You can't touch that. The police will need to see it."

I pull my arm from his grip. "Fine. But I'm going to review whatever else is in here."

"Liv - "

"If you don't like it, you can leave. That way, you don't have to lie."

"Why would I lie for you?"

"Okay, wrong choice of words; but you've been hiding my true story for twelve years. Or at least I believe you have been."

"What's that supposed to mean?"

"You're the one person next to Charlotte who knows my history and who Calvin's real father is."

"And you're concerned I told him?"

"I'm not aware of what you and Calvin talk about during, or after, Youth Group. Perhaps your conscience became more important than our friendship."

"I'm going to disregard the idea that you believe I don't value our friendship. I'd do anything for you and Calvin." He tries to take my hand, but I brush him away. "The more important thing here is that Calvin hasn't come to Youth Group in years. I thought you were aware of that."

"What? No! Why didn't you tell me?"

"I'm sure I've mentioned it." He ponders for a minute. "Come to think of it, I don't recall you asking about it."

"Oh sure, put it all on me. I'm a horrible mother for trusting my son when he said he spent his Wednesdays after school with you. Heaven forbid I make a mistake." I hyperventilate. It's been years since my last panic attack, but the tightened chest, heavy breathing, sweating and a heavy weight on top of me are undeniable.

"You're not a horrible mother. Trust me. I've seen horrible mothers. What I don't understand is why would Calvin have that note under the floor but keep the shoe box under his bed?"

"Perhaps he wanted me to find the shoe box and learn that he was planning on leaving."

"Makes sense. I'm going to go make us some tea. Then we can figure out our next steps. Promise me you will not touch that note."

I make an invisible cross over my heart and try to get my breathing under control.

When the stairs stop creaking and water clangs against the bottom of the kettle, I reach into the floor. Every voice in my head screams, 'Destroy the letter! Protect him!' I live with so many lies. What was one more?

I use a small bottle of vodka to push the note aside. It falls to the bottom of the makeshift cubby and I pray there's a simple explanation. I glance at the cover of a porn magazine, but leave it. It looks like the evolution of the Internet hasn't eliminated those. I sift through the rest of the hidden papers, and find news articles, websites, photos, all about William. And me.

The room spins as I get to my feet. Two years ago, this disheveled bedroom would have been spotless. I lean against the dresser, I close my eyes and wait for equilibrium. How did Calvin find these articles?

I realize John hasn't actually answered my question. He never said he hadn't told Calvin about William. I stomp down the stairs and find John setting a tray of tea on the coffee table. I drop the stack of papers beside the tray and grab the scruff of the front of his t-shirt. Taken by surprise, he doesn't resist as I push him against the wall.

"Did you tell Calvin about William?"

"What? Liv-"

"Stop avoiding my question. Did you tell him?"

The sides of his mouth dropped. "Yes."

I pull him away from the wall and slam him back against it, "WHEN?"

He grabs my shoulders and pushes me to the center of the room. I don't let go of him and he moves with me. "I didn't tell him the name of his real father. I wouldn't do that without asking you."

I loosen my grip and relieve some pressure from John's neck, but I'm still nose to nose with him. "Then what did you tell him?"

"Let's sit."

"I don't want to sit. I want answers. Now talk."

Shoulders tight, he backs away and looks towards the exit. Is he afraid of me? He should be. "Calvin came to me. A few months after his sixteenth birthday. He was asking questions about his father. But he kept calling him Leonard. I reiterated the story you had concocted, but he wanted more. He was persistent. So I added in a few details about William. Without telling him, it was William. I'm sorry."

"Why didn't you tell me? What if Calvin started asking me questions? How bad I would have looked. How bad do I look? What did you tell him?" The rage I have towards William boils below the surface. I pace the room, my eyes focused on John. One of a few people I placed my trust in and it seems he didn't deserve it.

"My reasons for not telling you are purely selfish. Yes, reverends can be selfish too. I enjoy our time together and I figured you'd be angry. Given your reaction tonight, I wasn't wrong. I feared you would pull away and that would be the end of our friendship. As for what I told him, well, I alluded to the human trafficking but a smaller scale. Not a global enterprise. I tried to rationalize that you didn't tell him because, as bad as his father was, you still wanted him to at least see him as a human being, no matter what his flaws. Not a complete monster."

"Oh, well, at least you explained to a sixteen-year-old why their mother had been lying to him for his entire life. Yep, that worked out great! And you're right,

I'm angry. Do you know how long it took me to trust you enough to even tell you an ounce of my story?"

"Five years," John mumbles.

"Five years! And that was only because I was spiraling out of control and desperate for help. Desperate to be an exemplary mother to Calvin. Now, twelve years later, I find out one of my best friends has been hiding something from me for two years. TWO YEARS, you neglected to tell me. All because, as you said, you were selfish. Thanks for that." Tears stream down my cheeks. The occasional drop stains the carpet where I walk.

"I'm really sorry. If it would make you feel better, you could punch me. I really need a nose job."

"Ha! I'm considering it." His joke can't stop my tears, but I have to give John credit. He always knows how to lighten the mood.

John wraps his arms around me. This time, I don't push him away. I stand there and cry. I cry until there are no more tears left. When I'm done, I wipe my cheeks and pick up the pile of papers. I don't know if I can fully trust John anymore, but in this moment of desperation, I can't revisit my past alone. Ten, fifteen years ago, I would have gone at all of this by myself. Not now. I'm exhausted from carrying my secrets for so long.

The cup of cold tea shakes faster with every article I read about William and Helen's trial. Accounts of the beatings and rapes that I, and others, experienced in Los Angeles. There are magazine articles that cover my sister Claire's rise to Chief Financial Officer at thirty, and her fall from grace only a few short years later. Thankfully, her gruesome death at the hands of William's brother, Adam, are not included in the stack. To my knowledge, only five people in the world had knowledge of what happened that night and I'm the only one still alive.

The wedding announcement for William and I has been clipped out of The Telegraph. Spiders dance along my arms.

The engagement is announced between William, eldest grandson of Lord Hammond (deceased), of Buckland, Portsmouth, and Olivia, youngest daughter of Mr. Jonathan and Mrs. Arlene Beaumont, of Toronto, Canada.

Blue flashing lights filter in through the living room windows and light up the room. I drop the announcement onto the stack of papers.

"That was quick," John says.

"They must have found her." I stop for a moment as Shaylynn's soft round face grows clearer in front of me. When it fades, I scramble to pick up all the papers. "Here, put these in your pants."

"Excuse me?"

"If they see these-"

"You can't. I can't-"

"We will. I left the note, but they can't see these. They'll assume Calvin is exactly like his father. A cold-blooded monster. They'll disregard any evidence they may find to the contrary."

"You don't know that."

"I do. The pressure to close a case involving the murder of a young girl is insurmountable. I had many friends buckle under the pressure and end up charging the wrong person. I can't let that happen."

KNOCK. KNOCK. "WOODHAVEN POLICE. OPEN UP."

"Take them!" I wave the papers at him.

Reluctantly, he shoves them around his torso, held in by his belted jeans. Once he pulls down his t-shirt, I run upstairs for my gun. I don't want them finding that either. Licensed or not.

Everything hidden on our persons, I open the door. DI Whitaker, Officer Cole and five others stand before me.

"Here's your warrant." DI Whitaker slaps it into my hand and walks past me. "Search everywhere!" No one speaks as they scatter throughout the house. DI Whitaker runs his hand along the living room door frame. "I expect you touched nothing?"

"I found a hidden compartment under the floor of his room, but I left it open for you." DI Whitaker blank facial expression doesn't change.

"Is that so? And I'm to believe you left it in the state you found it?"

"Yes. There is even a note a mother would have only been happy to hide. And I even left his laptop. Ask John." Now's the moment of truth. Will the man who wants to reclaim my trust lie for me?

CHAPTER NINE

OLIVIA

DI Whitaker looks at John, "Well? Is she telling the truth?"

Beads of sweat kiss the edge of John's widow's peak hairline. If DI Whitaker noticed, his face does not reveal it. I could have reheated the teapot in the time it takes John to answer.

"It's as she said. Except..."

"Except what?" DI Whitaker asks.

"We went through his entire room. Not just the floor. Oh, and it was a mess when we walked in. Teenagers, am I right?" John wouldn't be able to break the tension this time.

"Hmm. Well, we'll see what we find now, won't we?"

Officer Cole walks up to DI Whitaker and passes him a bag with a piece of paper in it.

"Is this the note you mentioned?" He turns the words towards us. I move to stand beside John. He'll need my support to make it through the potential minefield of lies.

She hurt me. Now I will hurt her.

"Yes," I say.

"You're right. It doesn't make your boy look good, now does it? I'm curious. Why not destroy it?"

I need to play to his ego so he'll stop focusing on us and I can get John out of here before the lies kill him. "You're smart, and I suspect thorough, you would have found out about it at some point. I would only cause more trouble for Calvin if they found me tampering with evidence."

DI Whitaker tries, but can't hide the smile my stroke of his ego creates. A uniformed officer heads out the front door with Calvin's laptop secured in a plastic bag. "Password for the computer?"

"I don't know."

"Really?"

"Dust it for prints. Mine will be on it, as I tried to get into it. But with no luck."

"You seem to be the most honest mother of a murderer, I mean potential murderer, that I've ever seen. You've also settled down since the last time I saw you."

John squeezes my shoulder. "Trust me, if you were here forty-five minutes ago, you would have seen a different Olivia. I'm pretty sure I have a few bruises."

"I didn't realize your services included being a stand-in punching bag," DI Whitaker says. His eyes burrow into John.

"This is an extenuating situation," John replies.

"We will be here a while. If you want to stick around you can, or you can head out and I'll call you, should you be able to enter your house again."

"Should? Why wouldn't she-" I take John's hand in mine.

"It's okay. I have no reason to believe anything happened to Shaylynn in this house. Let's just go. They'll let me back in a day or two."

We grab our coats and sit in John's car as some contents of Calvin's room, and the house, end up in the back of a van. My gun digs into my back. "I can't watch this anymore. Let's go. I'm sure Aunt Maud will let me stay with her."

"It's 4:30 in the morning. Do you want to wake her? Besides, how are you going to explain any of this to her? Especially all the papers living in my pants. Which itches like hell, by the way." He squirms in his seat as an officer positioned outside my front door watches.

"Hey, if my sweatpants would have held them, plus this, I would have hidden the articles myself." I discreetly pull out the gun while I put on my seatbelt.

"Where did you get that? Wait, that's what you ran upstairs for?"

"I had it before I came to Woodhaven. I didn't need DI Whitaker asking even more questions if they found it. Thank you, by the way. For that and for confirming my story with DI Whitaker."

"Do you think he believed us?"

"Hard to say. If I were him, I'd be skeptical. But there was nothing to support a lie, so it would be better to leave it for now and bring it up if it ever becomes a point of contention."

"Great. More lies. A favourite in my profession."

"Oh, the roads I could travel with that statement."

"Changing the subject. Why don't you stay with me?"

"Are you even allowed to have women stay in your home when they are not your wife?" I joke.

"I'm sure Mrs. Olson and the other ladies in her social group may have some choice words about it. But I don't care."

"Are you sure? They help pay your salary, and I bet Mrs. Olson can get you booted out of the church if she tries hard enough."

"Oh, she can try, but I can take her."

The reprieve from the stress and worry is nice. Even if it only lasts the two long and three short roads to John's. The prominent sandstone architecture featured in the front of my house continues to many of the cottages in town, including John's.

Lush vines cover half of the front face of the house. They hug the narrow white window frames. They stop short of the dark stone roof. The yellow door adds an unexpected pop of colour to the otherwise natural tones which surround it. A pale light filters out the half-moon window inset in the door's top.

Two small gardens of tulips grow beneath the bay windows of the main floor. The ladies of the town's horticultural society maintain the grounds for John. With as much help as he provides around my house, gardening is not a strength.

Inside the house, John places the stack of articles in a drawer of the barnwood table in the hallway. "You should get some sleep. I'll show you to your room."

We drag our feet up the refurbished two-hundred-year-old stairs. It's been a long night and as much as I know I need sleep, I need answers more. I don't want to keep John up any longer, so I'll wait until he's asleep before I continue my hunt.

John turns the crystal doorknob and reveals a basic, but inviting, bedroom. John had made the bed with military precision. "I promise this room's clean. Even if it has seen no visitors for a while. I'll be across the hall if you need me."

"Thank you. For everything."

His kind eyes say more than his words. "You're welcome. Now sleep."

"Yes, sir!"

He closes my door, and I monitor him through the keyhole. The door across the hall shuts. The shower water turns on. I wait for John to finish his shower. The faint light that emits from his keyhole extinguishes, and I sit still until I'm confident he won't emerge from his room. Millimeter by millimeter, I turn my door handle until the bolt releases. I inch the door open and tip-toe downstairs, grateful the old stairs don't creak.

I stand in front of the hallway table. The drawer resists opening and the rails squeak. My mouth slacks. Calvin's papers are gone. Was I so tired my brain made up the idea that John placed them there? Did he bring them upstairs with him? I didn't remember them in his hands.

The house is as silent as a graveyard at midnight. If John told Calvin about his father without asking me, maybe there was more to John than I realized. Charlotte's reluctant background check had revealed nothing. However, people who have secrets they want to keep hidden can do so. I did.

While I'm up, I'll take a quick look around John's office. Quench the idea his intentions are malicious.

Still on the tips of my toes, I make my way to John's office. The door's open. The room's dark. I flip on the light switch and almost faint.

"I told you to get some rest," John says.

Chapter Ten

Stranger

An aroma of nuts steams from my coffee cup while I listen to the horns of Big Band music ricochet off my walls. The coffee revitalizes me for the day ahead. The scent reminds me of the day I met Calvin, on his sixteenth birthday at the Coffee Shed. When he walked through the red framed door, the distance from where I watched him disappeared.

Calvin's raised shoulders hug his neck. Both hands clench the shoulder strap of his backpack. I stand and Calvin locks his eyes on me. A deep breath later and he's beside my table, unsure if he should sit down. His hands wring the backpack strap.

"Have a seat." I point across from me and he obeys. "Can I get you anything?"

"A pop would be fine. Please."

When I get back with Calvin's drink, the birthday card and article I ensured he received are on the table.

"I suspect you are wondering why I sent you that?"

Calvin nods, "And who you are."

"That piece of information will come in time. For now, you can call me M."

Calvin looks around the coffee shop as if he will find the definition of "M" in the faces of one of the other patrons. I'll have to explain it to him. "Like the head of MI6 in the James Bond books. Or movies?" Calvin didn't seem to register the information. "M conducted secretive work & employed Britain's masters of disguise."

"Oh. Why won't you tell me who you are?"

"I need to protect myself. From your mother. Yes, I knew your mother, and I don't think she would be happy that I'm unlocking the door to her, and your past. You cannot tell her about our visit."

"Why not?"

"She wouldn't allow any further visits, which I'm positive you will ask for. So if you want to hear about your real father, not this Leonard character your mom created, you will keep me, and our meeting, a secret."

Calvin leans over the table and lowers his voice. "How are you aware of Leonard?"

"My knowledge is vast. Do you want to learn about what your mother did to your real father?"

His eyes bulge. I have him.

"Drink up and I'll share with you some information I have about your parents."

Calvin's face contorts as I reveal how Olivia changed her last name; where she came from, and how she killed William on the side of the road. His transformation gives me about as much satisfaction as when I reflect on Olivia's time locked in the horse stables at Hammond Manor.

Months of dirt, cold, and agony. She deserved far worse living quarters. A grave. However, no one accepted my opinion on the matter.

Calvin's eyes flicker with fire upon hearing his mother killed his father. He can no longer control the volume of his voice. "She wouldn't do that!"

"I assure you she did. But that's enough information for now. Your mom will expect you home for dinner."

"Why would she kill my...him?"

"If I'm being honest, the family did some bad things. Some of them to your mother. However, I assure you she deserved the punishments she received. Had she left everything alone, your father would still be alive. I'd also have my family and we would all be prospering. I understand why, with your mother's past, she may not have wanted the luxurious life she lived; however, that doesn't justify keeping your father a secret from you." I pick up a thick manila envelope from the seat beside me. "Here, take these. It will help you understand what I'm telling you. But only your mother can answer why she killed your father."

Calvin takes the envelope full of selected news articles and stuffs it into his backpack.

As predicted, Calvin asks, "When can I see you again?"

"Same time next week."

"Next week? That long?"

"These meetings are to be kept a secret. If the people of Woodhaven see their prized football player leaving town all the time, there will be questions. Especially from Mrs. Olson. Who would be sure to tell everyone, including your mother? We don't want that, remember?"

"You've met Mrs. Olson?"

"Yes. And she can't keep a secret. If I'm going to help you understand who your family really is, then we need to be careful. So next week, same time. But let's meet down there by the docks."

Calvin looks out into the bay. Boats bob in the water, waiting for their sunrise wake up call.

"Fine." He grabs his backpack and starts towards the cafe door.

"Calvin?" He looks back.

"Happy Birthday."

Calvin manages a small smile and leaves.

An unstable tower of secrets teeters on destruction. A birthday card was all it took to knock it over. A card I had delivered by the last Hammond heir. Helen's son.

CHAPTER ELEVEN

OLIVIA

John sits in the vintage leather desk chair on the far side of the room. His arms move from the armrests to form a closed triangle on the desk. His customary black shirt and white collar has replaced his Ramone's t-shirt. I doubt he sleeps in those.

"I thought I told you to get some sleep." The jokester John is not present at this moment.

"How? But...You..." I stutter, searching for words.

"The handy thing about these old houses is that they sometimes contain hidden staircases."

Of course they do.

He continues, "Were you spying on me to make sure I didn't leave my room? That's not nice of a houseguest."

"I..." Fuck. There's no lie plausible enough for him to believe. "You know I'm not always nice."

"Touche." He rises from his chair, moves to the front of his antique desk and leans back against it. "What were you hoping to find in my office?"

"My plan wasn't to search your office. I was only going to look over Calvin's papers again. Maybe we missed something. But they aren't in the drawer of the hallway table."

"You noticed."

So I wasn't crazy. That's good. "Where are they?"

"Right here." He pats a stack of papers beside him. "But that doesn't explain why you were coming into my office."

Over the years, John has demonstrated he's a smart and observant man. I rationalized he liked me a little more than the other townsfolk. With everything going on, I wonder if it was something else. With only a small amount of sleep, he's still one step ahead of me. He reminds me of someone I spend every day trying to forget.

"Call me paranoid, but when the papers weren't where I remembered them to be, I wanted to make sure there was nothing else I should know about you. People in my life tend to be more than what they seem. Sometimes for the better and sometimes for the worse. Calvin trusts you as much as I do. I need to protect us both right now."

"Mistakes riddle people's pasts. I've made mistakes. It doesn't mean that I'm out to get you. If I was, do you think I would wait so long?"

"You would if you were playing the long game. Wait until I was finally feeling like my past was behind me."

A flash of recognition fires in his eyes. He's hiding something. I need to take control of the situation. "How did you know I would come into your office?"

"I doubted you would stay in your room, given you were without the papers. The kitchen is right under my bedroom and the front rooms contain creaky floors. Which I suspect you remember. So the only logical choice would be my office. It also has the bonus of having some private items of mine in here."

He's good. But I'm better. The Hammonds tried to take me on twice, and I won both times. If John's playing a game, it will be one I'll win. My peripheral vision locks onto an ivory carving of a cross on a table within a dashing distance. I can get to it before John if I need a weapon.

"I guess you should start your search." John steps away from his desk.

"You *want* me to search your office?"

"I have nothing to hide."

"Or you removed it while you waited for me to come downstairs. Like you did Calvin's papers. Did you even shower, or was that a distraction?"

49

"I was woken up by a call from the police around twelve thirty this morning, and rushed around town ever since, so yes, the shower was real. I've removed nothing from my office. Or hidden it in any secret compartments. There is a safe behind that lighthouse painting. I can unlock it."

Was he trying to distract me with kindness? I stare at him for a moment. His caring smile and kind eyes, normally comforting, put me on edge. If I take him up on his offer, what kind of friend does that make me? Do I care?

"I'm sorry, but I have to look. Calvin's future is on the line and right now I can only trust myself."

"I understand." He builds a fire in the large granite fireplace across from the desk. Afterwards, he unlocks the safe and waits in front of the fire while I rummage through his things.

The air's consumed by burning pine and awkwardness. I keep looking over my shoulder to find John focused on a book. Not once do I catch him monitoring me. His calmness compounds my nerves.

It doesn't take me long to go through the small room. The desk drawers reveal nothing relevant. I run my hands around the edges of the desk and find no hidden compartments. The pages of the books on the two bookshelves contain no secrets.

I leave the safe for last. I was already testing the strength of our friendship with my search. There's a sizable stack of money, different sizes and I estimate maybe twenty or thirty thousand pounds. There's also a deed for the property, in the church's name; John's passport; John's ordination papers; a medium blue suede box big enough to hold a necklace. The gold hinges of the blue box creak with the raising of the lid. A blue sapphire teardrop hangs from a string of alternating single diamonds with trios of blue sapphires. I'm about to close the box when my eye catches sight of a sliver of pale yellow peeking out from under the base. My thumb had been covering it. I rearrange my grip and lift the black velveteen base the necklace sits upon. I shake open the folded paper. A Certified Copy of an Entry of Birth from the General Register Office.

My heart stops when I read the names of John's mother.

Chapter Twelve

Olivia

Forename: Johnathan

Father's Forename and Surname: Harold Buckley

Mother's Forename and Surname: Mary Caldwell

My strength evaporates from my hands and the necklace, lid over bottom, crashes onto the hardwood floor and shatters into pieces. Jewels and casings bounce and roll in all directions. The paper flutters to the ground. The wall barely holds me up. I rest my forehead against it. The coolness of the night seeps through, but does not quench the heat that rises inside of me.

"Are you okay?" John's voice filters through a thick fog behind me.

Pushing myself off the wall, I fling around on my heels. Squatted on the floor, John's picking up the pieces of the necklace. He reaches for the paper. My strength resurfaces. I step on the paper before John's able to grasp it. My toes pull it towards me and I pick it up.

"It looks like I was right to only trust myself. This secret sat right under my nose and beside a nice pile of cash. Plan on going somewhere?"

"I'm not going anywhere. What are you talking about?"

"What am I talking about? Did you not think I would find this in my search? You must take me for some kind of fool. I trusted you more than anyone in this town and now..."

"What is that?" John reaches out his hand, palm up, and waits.

51

"Only proof that I will never be free from the Hammonds. Ever." Either I'm getting larger, or my surroundings are getting smaller as they close in on me. I push past John, take his keys from the dish on the hallway table, and run to his car. His footsteps echo behind me.

A strong grip cups my shoulder and spins me around. Both of John's hands now hold me firmly in place on his front lawn. My efforts to push him away are unsuccessful.

"Tell me what is going on!"

For someone calculated enough to wait for me in his office, he was utterly clueless at this moment.

"Who is your mother?" A sucker punch of words that frees me from his grip.

"But...I...She..."

"You're a fucking Caldwell. Like the one who helped Helen give me this!" I pull my hair back to reveal a faint H scar. Years of skin grafts removed 90% of it, but there's still evidence of that horrific event. The yellow glow of John's front porch lamp pulls the memory from the locked box I'd put it in. The cattle branding iron with its fiery yellow, orange and red H seared the side of my skin behind my ear. William's Aunt, Lady Helen Hammond's assertion of power still haunts my dreams.

"You don't understand-"

"Oh, I understand. You waited, gained my trust, and that of my son. Now you're playing some sort of sick game to get revenge. Is your plan to take away the one thing in this world that makes it worth living? Then try to run and avoid getting caught."

"Olivia, I swear I have no plans to hurt you or Calvin. Quite the opposite, actually. You're both family to me."

"Family! Yet you kept this enormous secret? Yes, yes, I did the same to Calvin, but this is different." What the difference was, I don't know, but it didn't matter. I won't be able to trust John again.

"Listen to me-"

"Nothing you say will help. William's eyes stare at me through Calvin and now...now Caldwell's stare at me from yours."

John grabs the car keys from my hand and tosses them into the bushes. "I won't let you leave until you hear me out."

"Sure, exercise your power to get what you want, despite the wishes of others. What are you going to do, lock me up in the shed in your backyard? Tie me to a chair until you weave your story?" I'm forty-nine years old, and will still fight with prowess for my life if I have to.

John rams me back against the car and presses the entire weight of his body against me. Anger fills his dark eyes. "You will listen to me. You have to!"

"I don't-" His hand covers my mouth. I try to fight back, but he has me pinned and is much stronger than I am.

"I didn't tell you about my mother because it's only a name on a piece of paper. As a baby, I'd been dropped off at a fire-hall and never knew my parents. The Reverends at St. Thomas' took care of all the paperwork for me to enter the seminary, so it wasn't until four years ago that I found out who they were. I needed a copy of my Entry of Birth to get a passport. I hadn't needed one before and was just as surprised as you when I received it."

My inaudible questions kiss his hand.

"I knew you would turn against me if I told you. Perhaps even leave town. Calvin means the world to you, and whether or not you believe me, you mean the world to me. I didn't want to risk losing you. I burned the document once I got my passport. How a copy found its way into my safe is beyond me. I didn't put it there. As for the money, it's what little savings I have. The way the markets crash every few years I avoid the banks and just keep cash on hand."

I search his eyes. Water wells in them and his chin quivers. I'm shaking. Confused.

"I'm going to remove my hand and step back. You can run, but I hope you stay and we can try to figure this out together. Something is going on here and I promise I'm not a part of it."

Released from his grip, I peel myself off the car.

I can't go home. The house is still under police control. Charlotte wasn't able to make it to town until the weekend. Aunt Maud wouldn't ask questions, she never did. However, she's been a part of this town for forty years. It would only be a matter of time until she's scorned for helping me. She doesn't deserve that.

Staying could be a trap.
Staying could help me find answers.

CHAPTER THIRTEEN

OLIVIA

Without warning, a bright white light in my cell flickers until it finds its solid rhythm. The drastic change in my surroundings sears my eyes. I cover my face with my arm until they can adjust.

I had slept minutes at a time, if that.

The long narrow flap on the metal cell door opens up like a table and a plastic tray is placed upon it.

"Eat up kid." A gruff voice says. All I see is a thick beard through the opening. "You'll be seeing Whitaker soon and there's no more food until lunch."

The latch to another cell opens, and another tray is delivered.

I pick up my tray and sit back down on the cement bench. Toast with butter. Nope, margarine. A sliced apple and lukewarm tea. I consume it all without registering the flavours.

My impatient fingers dance on my knees. I distract myself looking at the faded crude images occupants before me had somehow sketched onto the wall. Quite a few people are taking it up the ass. The metal door swings open just as I find an unflattering picture labeled DI Whitaker.

"Why are you smiling, kid? Find it funny being in here?" The same gruff voice stands before me. The trimmed beard belongs to a short squat man who protrudes from his uniform at every opening.

"No. It's just...never mind."

"Hands forward." Metal handcuffs squeeze my wrists as they interlock. "Let's go." Holding the chain of the handcuffs, he yanks me towards him.

I walk in front of the officer, down the same path I traveled yesterday. The scents of stale coffee and printed paper welcome me. Officers talk in groups around the station. They all watch me walk by.

Has Mom found a lawyer already? Or was DI Whitaker going to take another run at me with no one present? If he does, I will keep my mouth shut. I will only get myself in trouble if I say anything, and Shaylynn wouldn't want that.

When the interrogation room door opens, I'm comforted by the sight of Mom. She's wearing clothes I don't recognize. The comfort evaporates when my fury reminds me of her betrayal. With her is a large man dressed in a pressed suit. His square jaw clenches and he glares at me. I hope this scary man is on my side.

Mom steps forward and gives me a hug. "This is Ray Bower. He'll be your lawyer."

Thank God!

The man holds out his hand. I take it and he squeezes mine hard, then points for me to sit with the tip of his pen. I do what I am told.

"If I am going to help you, I need to know everything you know. We cannot be taken by surprise now, or heaven forbid there be one, at trial. Do you understand?" His voice is softer than his exterior, but not by much.

"Start from the beginning. And I mean the beginning. When you first met Shaylynn and everything up to last night."

I look over at the mirror.

"There's no one there. It's illegal to listen in and they, too, don't want any misstep with this. Now talk."

I glance at Mom, "It's okay. I called Aunt Charlotte and Mr. Bower comes recommended. We can trust him."

"But..." I pick at my remaining cuticles. There are things I don't want Mom to hear.

"I promise I won't get angry at anything you say. I want to help you come home. No matter what."

"What if I want to talk to Mr. Bower alone?" I whisper.

My mom's jaw drops slightly and her eyes glisten with tears. She wipes the shock off her face.

"She can wait outside, if you want her to," Mr. Bower responds.

"And you can't tell her what I say?"

"Not unless you give me permission. You can tell me what I may and may not share. I'm here for you. Not her."

I nod.

Hurt, Mom hesitates to get out of her chair. After a deep breath, she slides across it and hugs me. "I love you. Tell him everything, okay?" Then she's gone.

Mr. Bower has a note pad positioned on the table in front of him, and clicks his pen three times. "Take as much time as you need, and try not to leave out any detail you think might help."

A glass of water sits before me. I take a sip and begin.

"Shaylynn and I have known each other our entire lives. We both grew up in Woodhaven. But we didn't start hanging out until high school. She changed a lot the summer after eighth grade. She acted like she didn't care what anyone else thought of her. I loved that. I was always so worried about what everyone thought. My mom, teachers, Reverend John and, of course, the other guys on the football team."

"After a match, I was upset because I made a misplay which resulted in the winning goal for the other team. I found a bottle of vodka at home, went to the bluffs and started drinking. Out of nowhere, Shaylynn sat beside me, dangled her legs over the cliff and took the bottle out of my hand. Her confidence impressed me, and I couldn't say anything. We spent the night talking and when the bottle was empty, we stumbled to our homes. We've been best friends ever since. Do you really need me to go through every time we hung out? That's three years of daily stuff."

"How about I ask you some questions? The same ones the police will ask and go from there?"

"K."

"Were you and Shaylynn dating?"

"Um. Not exactly." Mr. Bower waits for me to continue. "I wanted to, but I was too scared to ask."

"Did anything sexual happen between the two of you? I need to know everything, remember? And I mean everything."

"We had sex a few times." I add, "Just to see what it was like."

"When was the last time you had sex?"

"A couple of days ago. We skipped the last period and went to my house while Mom was still at work."

"So her DNA will be on your bedsheets?"

"Yes." Shit! My heart's trying to break out of the jail of my chest.

"The police will try to use that against you. When they bring it up, let me do the talking. You look like you are going to shit a brick and I don't need you messing this up. Understand?"

Whoever this guy is, he would give DI Whitaker a run for his money. I think I'm going to like him.

"Now, what happened yesterday? From the first time you met with Shaylynn until you were arrested."

"I remember little."

"Try. I can't mitigate it if I don't know about it."

I inhale, close my eyes and I recount my day with Shaylynn. We spent our lunch hour behind the football field house. We hid there as people bullied Shaylynn for being what they couldn't be - herself. We met up after school, as usual and walked for hours around town. Neither of us wanted to go home.

I recall what I can about our time that night on the boardwalk. However, when I get to where we step into the forest, my mind goes blank. No matter how hard I try, I can't remember. "I'm sorry. I just don't know what happened."

"That's okay. It happens. Sometimes a person's brain protects itself by suppressing traumatic events. We can work on that. I suspect you don't have a very good poker face, so when presented with evidence, or a sequence of events that the police think may have happened, say nothing. Try to hide all emotion. Again, I will answer for you. If I need you to speak, I will ask you to. Does that work?"

I nod.

"Is there anything else I should know?"

"I don't think so."

"What about your relationship with your mom? Why didn't you want her in here?"

Ah man, I didn't want to talk about this. "We haven't gotten along for a couple of years. I can't trust her."

"Why?"

"Well, she never told me her last name is actually Beaumont, not Lyons. Then, she always told me my father's name was Leonard Dawson, when it's William Hammond. A human trafficker. She's lied to me my entire life."

"Well, that's one I haven't heard before. Is your mom aware you have this knowledge?"

"Yes."

"How long has she been aware?"

"Since last night."

"Noted. And this William Hammond. Do you know where he is now?"

"Dead. My mom killed him when I was a baby. Before we came to Woodhaven."

"Is that right? And how do you know this?"

"A friend told me. Gave me articles, his autopsy report, all kinds of stuff."

"Who is this friend?"

My hesitation doesn't go unnoticed.

"Do you want to protect your friend or yourself?"

"So...I just call them M. Like in the Bond films."

"A secretive friend. Those are never good. Where can I find this person?"

"We always meet around Coltam. But I don't think they live there."

"Why would you say that?"

"They always talk about having a long drive home." Mr. Bower's pen scribbles more words than I said.

"How long have you known this mystery person?"

"Two years. Since my sixteenth birthday."

"You've known someone for two years, but know nothing about them. Is that correct?"

I never thought of it that way. They wanted to use a code name so that Mom wouldn't find out. They thought it was safer that way.

"Do you know anything about this person that might help me find them?"
I shrug.

"Does this person know Shaylynn, or have any reason to hurt her?"

"No! They knew Shaylynn, but they would never hurt her. We're all friends."

"I know you are just a kid, but friends don't hide their names from each other. How old do you think they are? Is it another teenager? Adult? Older adult?"

"Older adult, fit. Looks better than a few athletes I watch."

"Okay. I'll have many more questions later about this friend of yours. Shifting gears, what can you tell me about a note found under the floorboard that said, 'You hurt me, now I will hurt you'."

They found the note! That means they found all the articles about my father. And my mom. This isn't good. I'm so stupid. I should have gotten rid of everything.

"Calvin, the note."

"I wrote it a couple of weeks ago. After the school year finished, Shaylynn and I were going to run away to London. It was part of a package with all the news articles about my parents. Do they think it was for Shaylynn? Oh god, no, it was for my mom. My mom, not Shaylynn."

"I see. I need to ask you one more question before DI Whitaker comes in here. Did you kill Shaylynn, or have any reason to believe you did?"

"No. I don't know. Maybe."

"Why maybe?"

"I remember us fighting in the woods. I have these flashbacks of her running away from me. She looks so scared."

Mr. Bower's voice raises a little, "Remember when I said you need to tell me everything. This is part of everything you should have told me when we talked about last night. What did you fight about?"

"I don't remember. I promise I'm not hiding anything else."

"If you are, they will find out." He waves at someone on the other side of the clear glass window in the door.

A moment later, DI Whitaker walks in carrying a folder that hugs a stack of papers. Officer Cole follows behind with a box. I didn't have to see what was inside to know I wouldn't like it. Mom peeks her head around the corner. The circles under her red eyes have gotten darker and her shoulders hang low.

DI Whitaker takes care of the formalities with the recording and his first question knocks the breath right out of me.

"Why are your fingerprints on a 10 inch knife covered in Shaylynn's blood?"

Chapter Fourteen

Calvin

D I Whitaker pulls out a large knife, secured in a plastic bag, and places it on the metal table in front of me. My hands tremble and are sweaty. I hide them under the table and between my legs.

I don't remember having a knife in the forest. But, in my dream, I stabbed Shaylynn, so there had to have been a knife. What have I done? I run my fingers through my hair.

Mr. Bower says, "My client cannot recall the events of that night and that includes any knowledge of a knife."

"His fingerprints are all over it, and he's still claiming he can't remember?"

"Where was this knife found?" Mr. Bower asks.

"In the brush about five hundred meters from Shaylynn's body."

Mr. Bower writes some notes. His handwriting is illegible, so I can't see what he's written. "Were there other prints on the knife?" he asks.

"That is not the point of the question. I want to know how Calvin's prints got on it."

"If there are other prints, then there are other suspects."

"You want to go down that road? Fine. Is there any reason your mother, whose prints were under yours, would want to kill Shaylynn?"

"Mom...what?"

"The knife is from your kitchen, Calvin. Now either you or your mom used this knife to stab a beautiful young girl, multiple times. Which of you was it?"

My mouth's dry and white film forms around the corners. I'm out of water. None of this makes any sense. My reflection in the two-way mirror takes away the superstar football player and replaces him with a feeble boy.

"I-"

"My client cannot recall the events of that night, and that includes any knowledge of a knife."

A silent stare down between the two men continues until Officer Cole pulls out a photo of my blue bed sheets. She coughs. DI Whitaker glances down. "And what about the stains found on these sheets? What can you tell me about those?"

"Calvin admits that he and Shaylynn had sex. Consensual sex, as recently as Thursday."

"We shall see if the rape kit confirms or disputes that. Tell me about your missing running shoe. We found it in a trash bin along High Street, where Mrs. Olson found you. Covered in blood spatter."

Why would I get rid of my shoe? When did I get rid of it? I ran into Mrs. Olson almost as soon as I exited the forest. Brain, start remembering!

DI Whitaker continues. "The thing is. Your left shoe had just as much blood on it as your right one. Why get rid of one and not the other?"

"My client cannot recall the events of that night, and that includes any knowledge of his shoes."

"No knowledge of his shoes. Right. Do you have any knowledge of any of the events of last night?"

"No," I mutter.

"Ahh, he speaks. Glad to see you haven't lost your voice, but only gained a lawyer's."

"This note, 'You hurt me, now I will hurt you.' What is this about?"

Mr. Bower nods for me to speak. "I wrote it for my mom."

"Is that so? And what did your mother do to hurt you?"

I'm confused. They should know what she did. The newspaper articles about my father's trial show pictures of her. Why are they asking me this?

Mr. Bower must have the same questions as he steps in. "The reason my client wrote that note to his mother is not relevant."

"Oh, I think it's very relevant. Did you kill Shaylynn as some sort of payback for your mother?"

"What? No!"

Mr. Bower rests his hand on my arm. "Calvin, let me do the talking."

"Did your mom try to stop you and Shaylynn from being together and you decided that if you can't be with her, no one could? Or maybe your mom killed Shaylynn, but you tried to cover it up."

"We're done here!" Mr. Bower stands and stuffs his belongings into his briefcase.

"In that case. Officer Cole."

"Calvin Lyons, you are under arrest for the murder of Shaylynn Taylor. You do not have to say anything. But, it may harm your defense if you do not mention, when questioned, something which you later rely on in court. Anything you do say can be given as evidence." She grabs my arm, pulls me out of my chair, and walks me out of the room towards the holding cells.

My mother stands when I exit the interrogation room and comes towards me. Reverend John is beside her.

"What's going on? What's happening?" Mom asks.

DI Whitaker addresses her, "You should say your goodbyes now. We've charged him with murder, and they will transport him to prison later today."

"You can't. He didn't do this."

"All evidence points to the fact he did. I'm sorry, Ms. Lyons, but unless you have another explanation for what happened, your son could go to prison for a long time. Given the severity of the situation, we will keep him in a regular prison."

My mother's screams follow me down the long narrow hall. I can't turn around. Despite everything, I don't want to see the pain I've caused her. I step into the same cell as before, and the door creaks but stops short of closing. I turn around and Officer Cole stares at me.

"What?" I ask.

"I know you couldn't have done this." Her green eyes are soft.

"Excuse me?"

"I've watched you grow up. You're too good of a kid to hurt someone like that. Especially Shaylynn. Everyone around town knows you were in love with her."

"They do?"

"But that will not help you. You've got to remember if you want to get out of here. DI Whitaker has zeroed in on you and the evidence isn't helping. I know I'm not a detective, but everything's lining up just a little too nicely. Something else is at play here."

"What?"

"Not what. Who."

CHAPTER FIFTEEN

STRANGER

A large crowd gathers outside the Woodhaven police station. The red brick building reminds me of a traditional army barracks. Unassailable construction and nothing fancy to look at. The barred windows would let no one in or out.

My contact inside the police force gave me the heads up that they would announce an arrest in the Shaylynn Taylor case. I'm pleased the turnaround time between Calvin's arrest and the charges has been swift.

My anonymous tip to news stations paid off. News vans, all the way from London, take up the length of the road in front of the station. It's the first time I've seen mainstream news in this part of the country. My plan for revenge will reach the homes of millions.

Reporters gather in the first three rows and residents stand six rows deep behind them. I position myself in the back to observe it all. It's no surprise Olivia is absent.

She will become an outcast in this town within the hour. Turned away everywhere she goes. The bell over the front door of Word Haven will never ring. With her business failing, her son convicted of murder, and rejected by the town, Olivia will spiral into darkness. At that moment, I will reveal the master of her demise. A face she prays will never return. Yet, here I stand.

Each step I take cracks the foundation of the trust Olivia has in those around her. Just days ago, shrouded in darkness and bushes, the lenses of my binoculars captured the moment Olivia found the paper I had left in Reverend John's safe. He'd gotten rid of his copy, but I needed Olivia to find it in his possession. The fight that ensued should have inflamed the distrust that always lives in Olivia. Somehow, Reverend John extinguished it enough for Olivia to continue to stay with him. It wasn't part of the plan, but I would adapt. I don't understand why she stayed. She hated the Hammonds and the Caldwells with every ounce of blood inside her. He must have said something to her to make her stay, but his back was to me so I couldn't hear or read his lips.

The moment the car keys landed beside me in the bush, I thought they would find me. I crawled back and hid behind the wide trunk of a tree, ready to run, should I need to. However, both ignored the keys and the nearby observer.

I watched them a little longer, but all fighting had ceased. I lurked outside the office window while they went through what looked like news articles. They had to be the ones Calvin kept in his secret compartment under the floor. I, too, had gone through his hiding place, amongst other things, during one of my visits to Wilkes Cottage when the occupants were out. I had hoped the police would find the articles and then question who Olivia was and all of her secrets. It wasn't integral to my plan. I'll make sure the police learn who Olivia really is. This town will never trust her again.

The clicking of cameras brings my attention back to the present. DI Whitaker struts out of the police station and the murmurs of the crowd quieten. DI Whitaker stands with authority on the top step, behind a podium erected for the occasion. The size of the crowd does not phase the small-town detective.

"Thank you all for coming. I am Detective Inspector Daniel Whitaker, lead investigator on the Shaylynn Taylor case. I will make a brief statement and then take some questions. On Saturday, June 15th, seventeen-year-old Shaylynn Taylor's body was found in Woodhaven forest. She had been stabbed six times."

Gasps erupt from the surrounding townsfolk. The reporters keep silent. They've been witness to press conferences like this before.

"We've charged Calvin Lyons, of Woodhaven, with the murder of Shaylynn Taylor. We ask that you respect the Taylor family and allow them time to grieve in private. I will now take a few questions."

He selects a female reporter in the front row.

"It has been four days since Shaylynn's death. Would you say you completed a thorough investigation to ensure you arrested the right person?"

I don't like this reporter. I won't call her with the next tip.

"The Woodhaven police force takes this case seriously. We've worked day and night, and have filed charges against the accused based on conclusive evidence." DI Whitaker points to another reporter.

"Has the accused confessed?"

"No. However, as you know, murderers rarely do. One more question."

"Even though Mr. Lyon's been arrested, how can you assure the residents of Woodhaven that they are A - safe, and B - that the suspect was working alone?"

Waves of whispers travel through the crowd. They hadn't considered the fact Calvin may have had an accomplice. Fear for themselves grows with every passing second. DI Whitaker wipes the sweat from his balding hairline. He's asked the questions every officer hates to receive. Questions that don't always have a guarantee for their answer.

"I can assure everyone in Woodhaven that they are safe. There is no evidence to support that another perpetrator was involved. Thank you." DI Whitaker returns to the police station. The reporters toss questions at his back.

He's not wrong. The town is safe. I have no qualms with any of them.

Chapter Sixteen

Calvin

I wonder if television shows about prison are accurate? Will the first night really be the hardest? Will someone try to teach me a lesson about who is in charge? If they do, they will be in for a lesson of their own.

I close the few doors still open into my true self when the police car enters the prisoner drop-off garage. Any fear I had is gone. Any longing to crawl into a hole and die, gone. I need to be strong.

The guards who process me are firm, but nicer than I thought they would be. I'm still a little manhandled, but they do not hose me down with ice cold water. I take a regular shower, succumb to a very unpleasant body search, and put on the blue sweatshirt, pants, and slip-on shoes they provide.

I'm led to my cell, and the eyes of the other prisoners watch as I pass. Some whistle or toss taunts of late night visits. I doubt anyone knows why I'm here and I'll use that to my advantage. Whether or not I killed Shaylynn, those around me only have to suspect I did.

The first attempt to put the new guy in his place comes at dinner. Despite eating little in the past few days, I'm not hungry. Knowing I need the energy, I force down half the meatloaf and potatoes before the unease of my stomach tells me to back off.

I'm tempted to keep my wooden spork and see if I can convert it to a weapon, but I'm halfway out of my seat when I become distracted by a colossal figure who casts a shadow over me and my food tray. "Our food is not good enough for you, pretty boy?"

"The food is fine. I'm not hungry."

"Is that so?" He bends over the table. "I think you should finish it."

"Well, I think I'm finished." I stand and match his glare. I don't care that I'm smaller, I won't back down.

The scraping of cutlery ceases. Silence fills the cafeteria. The boiling water from vats on the stoves in the galley kitchen is the only sound. Even the prisoners serving food to arriving inmates, and those waiting for their food, stop to watch.

Knuckles collide with my eye. My food tray flies into the air as the force of the punch knocks me to the ground. I scramble to my feet, kick the tray out of the way, and ram my shoulders into the guy's stomach. I push him back onto a nearby table.

Unprepared for retaliation, I land a few hard punches before he throws me off of him. We square off, waiting to see who will make the next move. I block out all thoughts of the boy my mother wants me to be, focus on my target, and take a swing.

He dodges and hits me upside the head. Ringing fills my ears. Still standing, I pretend to punch with my right hand, which he blocks and land a hard punch in the ribs with the left. I pick up my used food tray.

"Look at this pretty boy, he thinks he can take me." The crowd around us laughs. "Come on, then, I barely felt that last punch. Let's see what you can do with the tray."

A familiar rage builds inside of me. The surrounding room disappears, and it's just me and the bully. I jump onto the chair, then the table, and the tray crashes down over his head. He falls to his knees. I jump down and smash the back of his head. Each hit brings him closer to kissing the food-littered floor. Blood trails down the back of his head.

An arm hugs my chest and my knees are taken out from under me. I hit the floor hard and my arms are pulled tight behind me. The room around me comes into focus. An officer checks the unconscious inmate. Handcuffs clamp onto my wrists, and I'm pulled up to my feet and dragged out of the room.

Everyone in the cafeteria, a room of stone statues, watches me leave.

Let's see if anyone else tries to come after me.

After a tongue-lashing from the Superintendent about prison behaviour and my courtyard privileges being stripped for a week, I'm returned to my cell. It is nicer than the one at the station, but still bare bones and cold.

Men returning from wherever it was they had been, peer inside my open door. Some mumble to the person beside them, others keep walking. I feel like the newest animal at the zoo that everyone's flocking to see. Some people come for repeat viewings as they circle the common area.

I sit on the foot of the bed, in full view of the common area outside my door, and make myself as big as possible. I need them to fear me enough to stay away from me. I don't want to make friends. All I want is to figure out what happened to Shaylynn. What I may have done to her.

Whatever anger and hatred took over my body in the cafeteria is becoming too familiar. For as long as I can remember, I was always angry. It just sat there, like I think contentment does for everyone else. I never understood why it was there and I do my best to hide it. No one else I knew was angry all the time.

As I got older, the anger grew within me. Learning about my real father brought it to the surface. Ever since my sixteenth birthday, I could not put a lid on the ever-present desire to scream. M was right to tell me the truth, but nothing has been the same since. My burgeoning anger causes fights with my teachers and teammates. They do nothing wrong, they're just in the wrong place when my fuse goes off.

I try to bottle up my anger until I'm on the football field or I can go for a long run. Hanging out with Shaylynn also helped. She could always tame my temper. Even if it was only for an hour.

That's why I don't understand why I would have killed her. She was the only thing that made me feel normal. Why would I take that away?

The events of that night are a blur. How did my running shoe end up in garbage on High Street? It wasn't in my hands when I was running out of the forest, was it? Why can't my stupid brain remember what happened?

And the knife? How did I even get it out of my kitchen? I hadn't left the house with it. Or at least I don't think I did. Why would I? I avoid my house, and my mother, as much as possible. I'm confident we didn't end up at the house at any point.

Then there are my dreams. Every night Shaylynn is running away from me, terrified. I finally catch up to her. My hand is on her shoulder. Her mouth opens wide, as though I punched her. We look down and there is blood pouring out of her.

Dreams can be wrong.

They have to be.

CHAPTER SEVENTEEN

OLIVIA

MURDERER in red spray paint, smashed eggs caked on windows, trees filled with toilet paper and a front yard full of trash welcomes me home. For a town that touts community and togetherness, they become vipers against those they no longer deem worthy. My son's being convicted by the residents of Woodhaven before a trial even begins.

The inside of the house looks no better. I was joking when I invited DI Whitaker to toss the place. The only items that remain where I left them are the wall-mounted television and large appliances. The contents of drawers and closets are littered across my floors.

"It looks like a bloody tornado went through your house, but left the walls standing," John says.

"I've lived in worse conditions." A messy house was nothing compared to the squalor of my first residence when the Hammonds kidnapped me. The filthy walls, fluid-stained mattresses littered with drugged women, and buckets for toilets made the disarray of my home look like a palace. At least I can control the environment inside my house.

"I'll start with the outside," John says, "just point me to a bucket, scrub brush, and some soap."

"Provided they have not moved them, you'll find them in the kitchen closet." I'm still cautious of John's motives, but over the past four days, there have been no more red flags. Either he hides them well, my bullshit radar has rusted over the years, or I have nothing to worry about. For now, I'm keeping a potential enemy close.

The rest of the day is grueling with all the cleaning. I have slept little and my body is reminding me of that. When I slept, I saw Calvin and William plan the expansion of the Hammond Empire. An amiable and evil father/son relationship.

Multiple times a day, I have to remind myself that Calvin isn't William. Doubt creeps into each reminder.

Little sleep, and a matching consumption of food, means most of my energy is spent within twenty minutes of cleaning, but I push through. I'm tempted to pack the essentials like clothes, toiletries and photos in boxes, ready to move on a whim. I could leave the rest where the officers tossed it. However, I don't want the nosy Mrs. Olson, or anyone else in this town, to think they've gotten the better of me. This town is Calvin's home. We'll only leave if our lives are at risk.

John's cleaning is interrupted multiple times by bombardments from townsfolk, whom I'd never seen walk up the hill to my house. They share how distraught they are that their beloved Reverend's helping the mother of a murderer. To ensure I can hear how they feel, from inside my house, they shout. They believe John should be the one guiding the Taylors through the loss of their daughter, not his superior, even though they appreciate the Bishop's presence. But the Bishop doesn't know the family like Reverend John does.

John handles each criticism the same way, quoting 1 John 4:20 "Whoever claims to love God yet hates a brother or sister is a liar. For whoever does not love their brother and sister, whom they have seen, cannot love God, whom they have not seen."

The lace curtains cannot hide the lashings he deals the visitors. God help me, but I take pleasure in their comeuppance. Their faces are often frozen and eyes shifting while they try to come up with a rebuttal. None found, they storm away.

With the inside of my house now in a semi-livable state, I venture to see the progress made on the outside. The blood-red MURDERER is more of a faded pink, but still legible.

"I'm going to need some heavy-duty cleaner to take this spray paint off."

"Don't bother. The culprits will come back a few more times before this whole thing is over."

"Are you sure? I don't mind."

"I'm sure."

"You look exhausted."

"I am. But I need to see Calvin. If he will let me. I still can't believe he wouldn't let me be there with his lawyer." The dams break and I collapse into John's arms. "How is this happening? Calvin couldn't have killed that girl. He just couldn't. Right?"

"He loved Shaylynn. He had no reason to kill her."

"Yet, he's kept so many secrets from me. What else is he hiding?"

"I know you don't want to hear it, but we need to trust God will guide us and keep Calvin safe. Charlotte said she would be here tomorrow. She'll have the results of what she's been able to find out about the case, as well as her searches for anyone nearby who may have worked for the Hammonds. For now, let's get you cleaned up to see your son. I don't know if they would even let you in, looking and smelling like this."

I clench the steering wheel and stare at the white and red brick building. A battering ram wouldn't be able to penetrate the large red metal doors. The last time I visited a prison was when Calvin was lying in a baby carrier, only a few months old. The same red brick made up the walls of both places. I hope the same monsters don't reside in each.

Fearless birds fly around like they are on a roller coaster, while I try to summon the courage to see my son, a Hammond by blood, who seems to be following in that family's footsteps. All of my pent-up anxiety and frustration bubbles out. I slam my hands against the top of the steering wheel.

How did I let this happen? I should have tried harder to find out why Calvin and I became enemies. Maybe then, he wouldn't have been out so late with Shaylynn and everyone would be fine.

I should have told him about William! I punch the dashboard so hard my little finger stings and no longer wants to bend. My anger numbs the pain. All my life, I've never been able to protect the people I love. I've failed again.

Calvin sits inside this cold, dark place, full of God knows what kinds of people, because of me. He's right, this is all my fault.

I've prayed every day, for the last eighteen years, that Calvin would differ from William; I prayed the facial features were the only resemblance. For sixteen years I had hope. Then came the anger and secrets. I'm desperate to believe Calvin couldn't have killed anyone. Not like that. Not...like a Hammond.

KNOCK, KNOCK.

I jump in my seat and put down my window.

A guard leans against my car and lowers his head. "Ma'am, are you waiting for someone? Or coming in? You've been out here for an hour and we can't just have you sitting around the parking lot."

"I'm sorry. Yes, I'm coming in." I gather up my phone, wallet, and keys and step out of the car.

I go through security in a daze and follow the same guard to the visiting area. The circular metal table and attached seats are cold. Both to the touch and to the eyes. I wait.

Hushed and loud conversations surround me. Families embrace and chat, while others huddle over the table to create some privacy.

Calvin has barely spoken to me in two years and didn't want me present when he spoke with Mr. Bower. Would he even want to see me now? I need to see him. I need to wrap my arms around him and tell him I will fix this.

I will find out the truth.

Something will point to the fact someone else killed Shaylynn.

CHAPTER EIGHTEEN

OLIVIA

The boy who walks through the door into the visitation center is unrecognizable. His eyes are colder than normal, which is saying something. He stands with his shoulders back and head held high. The bruises covering his face and knuckles mask the son I remember.

He ignores my outstretched arms.

"Calvin, I'm sorry I-"

"Don't. It's too late for apologies. You lied to me my whole life. That's unforgivable. I only agreed to see you because Mr. Bower is coming too. You're going to meddle in everything, like you always do, so let's just wait for Mr. Bower to show up."

"I'll fix this, I promise." I reach out for his hand. He pulls away.

"I doubt it."

Tears gather in the bottom of my eyes and I pinch the bridge of my nose to stop them from flowing.

For ten minutes, Calvin and I sit in silence. A pop can dropping to the bottom of a vending machine startles us. Calvin picks at his fingers and avoids my gaze. I watch my little boy fade further and further away from me.

A guard comes and ushers us to a private room where Mr. Bower is waiting, his brown leather bag propped against the table leg beside him. A yellow legal pad and silver pen are aligned in front of him.

Calvin, arms crossed, leans up against a corner of the room and I take the seat opposite Mr. Bower. The seat beside me is empty. I repulse my son.

"Calvin," Mr. Bower says, "I'm glad you reconsidered allowing your mother to take part in these conversations. It will make everything easier with her here. However, if there is anything you do not wish to speak of in front of her, we can ask her to step outside and invite her back when you are ready. Does that work for you?"

An inaudible gruff reply comes from the corner.

As hard as it is, I keep my questions to myself while I'm filled in on the details of Calvin's interrogation with DI Whitaker.

"Ms. Lyons-"

"Beaumont," says Calvin.

"Excuse me?" Mr. Bower asks.

"Her real last name is Beaumont, remember?"

"I don't have time to deal with your family squabbles. I will happily charge you for the extra time to navigate them. However, why don't we focus on what's important? Not your mother's name."

Another gruff noise spills out of Calvin.

"Given your previous line of work, I suppose you have questions?"

"Yes. Do we, I mean you, have witnesses that can corroborate that Calvin never went home after school, and therefore couldn't have gotten the knife? I would have noticed if he came home while I was there, and I didn't see or hear him all night."

"We do, until about ten o'clock. But after that, witnesses are sporadic and it gives him, or them, plenty of time to get to and from your house before Shaylynn dies. When was the last time you used the knife?" He pulls out a printout from a kitchen store website that shows a set of knives that matches what I have at home. He points to the largest one in the set.

"I only use it to carve a chicken or roast. Calvin and I haven't eaten together in a while, so I stopped making those meals. I don't remember the last time I used it. I don't remember the last time I saw it. It's not something I pay attention to."

"Calvin, I know we've gone over this, but when was the last time you used or saw it?" Mr. Bower asks.

"I don't remember. I never cook, so I had no reason to use it," Calvin responds.

"If Calvin didn't come home that night, perhaps whoever killed Shaylynn took the knife prior to that night?" Fear tickled my skin at the thought someone had been in my house. Someone intending to kill.

"The next question on everyone's mind is how did Calvin's bloody fingerprints get on the knife? Calvin, your memory loss is not generating any favours in this department. Have you remembered anything new since I last saw you?"

Calvin shakes his head, "No."

"In that case, I will keep digging. What other questions do either of you have, before I move on to the present results of the investigation?"

"I suppose the lack of witnesses also means we can't figure out why they only found one of Calvin's running shoes in the garbage and not both of them? If I was getting rid of evidence, I would have tossed all of it. Both shoes and his clothes."

"All very good points, and ones I am looking into. I'm still waiting for the discovery package of physical evidence so that I can have my own experts scrutinize everything. Questions?"

"I'll hold off until the end." I have two burning questions but I'm not sure if I want to ask them with Calvin present.

"The particulates under Shaylynn's fingernails match Calvin's DNA. This includes hair and skin."

I close my eyes and hang my head. Would any good news come out of this meeting?

"So with that, the knife, your clothes and the note - no matter if, you say you intended it for your mom - everything points to your guilt, Calvin."

"Thanks, Captain Obvious," Calvin grunts from the corner.

"Calvin! He's trying to help you. You could be a little more considerate."

"Like you were considerate all those years? You lied to me." A knife pierces my heart. "You heard him. I'm guilty. He's not saying anything we aren't thinking."

Mr. Bower rubs his temples. "I didn't say you're guilty. I said the evidence points to you being guilty. It doesn't look good. Bleak, but I have come back from more disheartening situations than this. We just need to keep looking. And you need to remember what happened."

"You don't think I haven't tried? There's nothing else to do here but try. All I want is to know if I did or didn't kill my best friend. At least then I'll know if I'm a monster like my father!"

I feel a slight relief. At least he doesn't look up to William.

"I appreciate how hard you're trying, but we are running out of time. Given the national attention this case is getting, a trial will start soon. I want to help you as best I can, but I need those memories. I'm going to arrange for a therapist to visit you. See if we can loosen the grip your memories have on their hiding place."

"Whatever." Calvin slumps down to the floor.

"Mr. Bower, I have another question. Is it safe for my son to be here? Look at him."

"I spoke with the Superintendent and Calvin won a fight against one of the larger men in here. Knocked him unconscious with a plastic tray. I think he'll be fine."

Calvin has gotten into a few scraps, but nothing this violent. My son is transforming into a monster all because I tried to protect him, by withholding the truth. If I don't fix this soon, I fear I'll lose him forever.

"Now, I haven't been able to track down this friend of yours-"

"Friend? What friend?" I ask.

"I'd like her to leave."

"Let me help. Please!"

"We all agreed if Calvin didn't want you here, you would wait outside. Let's respect his wishes."

My chair drags along the stone floor. Like a sloth, I make my way to the door. Maybe he'll change his mind. Calvin avoids my eyes. "I'll be right outside when you need me."

The only thing I can see is Mr. Bower through the window. The veins in his neck throb, but he keeps calm. Twenty minutes later he opens the door and I'm about to step inside when Calvin walks past me and up to the guard.

"We're done. Take me back to my cell."

"Calvin?"

No response. The gate buzzes open and he walks away. He doesn't look back.

Mr. Bower speaks over my shoulder, "He's got a lot of anger in him. I see it all the time, but he'll come around. He just needs time."

"Time he doesn't have."

Mr. Bower tilts his head, places his hand on my lower back and leads me out of the prison.

In the parking lot, I ask "Who is this friend? Do they know anything about Shaylynn's murder?"

"I'm sorry Ms. Lyons. Calvin has explicitly asked me not to divulge that information. Just know that he and I are working very hard to determine if this friend knows anything that can help. I have talented people working with me. We'll find them."

"Do you think my son did this?"

"My business is to build a defense for my client. Not determine their innocence. Try to get some rest. Once this trial starts, your life will become, well, a nightmare." Moments later, his BMW disappears out of the gate.

The barred windows of the prison taunt me. Somewhere in there is my son. Angry and alone. Somewhere out here is someone Calvin doesn't want me to find out about

Chapter Nineteen

Stranger

The summer wind whistles against the stone cliffs. My evening jog relaxes my mind, and allows me to focus my thoughts on what I need to do next to destroy Olivia. The attention is on one suspect. Calvin. The Crown prosecutor has taken the bait and expedited the trial. I need to add the final touches to the next piece of evidence.

The salty air kisses the back of my neck as I jog home to get to work.

A flat, rectangular box sits on my front step. No label.

I'd be more concerned if I wasn't expecting it, however, Buck was dropping off a new laptop for me. Such a silly nickname, Buck. The people who raised him gave it to him because he loved playing cowboy as a child. It's stuck with him through adulthood. I shouldn't reinforce it, however I have more important things to worry about than a name.

I've tried to avoid using a computer to make my plan for Olivia's demise a success; however, it was inevitable I would need one. I've been switching laptops every couple of months, to ensure the digital footprint I needed to make was not easily found.

After I clean myself up, my knife cuts through the seal on the package. I plug in the laptop and turn it on. Buck's already set everything up for me, so I get to work.

My fingers race along the keyboard. My cursor hovers over the 'post' button. I double check that I've changed the date and time on my computer. My research says it will reflect the same on the post, and it's worked for the last ones I put up. All dated differently, even the ones I posted on the same day.

Click.

Posted.

I text my contact at the police station to ensure they find my diary entries. "Found something for you. Check out www.Shayslife.com."

Calvin won't leave me alone. So we had sex a few times. Big deal. It doesn't mean I'm his girlfriend. Friends have sex all the time, no strings attached. I don't get why he's been so clingy the last few months. I've asked him to stay away from me after school, but he won't stop harassing me.

The anger in him I used to tame won't stay locked away anymore. It's getting worse than in the previous entries I've made. Much worse. He was so mad that I wouldn't hang out with him after school that he punched a tree I was leaning against. I thought his fist would hit my face.

The other night I was walking by myself. I needed to get away from another night of my parents fighting, and he came out of nowhere. He acted like it was normal running into me across town. The part of town he and I never went to. I swear he's stalking me.

I told him to leave and then we fought. He bruised my wrist from squeezing it so hard when he wouldn't let go.

He even yelled at me, "You can't do this to me! I'll hurt you for this."

I was being nice for still hanging out at school, but I'm going to cut him off completely. He doesn't have other friends, so I feel bad. But I can't be around someone like that. Someone whose eyes glow with an anger that terrifies me.

An anger that makes me think he could kill me.

Three dots appear on the screen, disappear and reappear. "Got it."

I should be elated and anticipatory, yet the veins in my neck throb with anger. Every piece of the puzzle I put together only adds to my hatred for Olivia. The closer I get to her demise, the more I want to face her head on. Show her she couldn't get away from me.

The Taylors will believe their daughter wrote it. So will the police and the rest of the town.

A cursor on a blank document taunts me. *What harm will one note do? Let Olivia know she's being watched. It'll drive her mad.*

My hands are out of my control, and words appear on the page. Keys clatter. Mouse buttons click.

The wheels of the printer purr as they warm up. A piece of paper gets sucked out of the tray and lies face down on top of the machine, warm to the touch.

Like a robot, I fold the note around some photographs. I tuck the note into an envelope and turn back to the laptop. I use a copy of one photo and place it in the middle of a new document. Below it, I put an image of Olivia Beaumont the day she testified against William. I make sure the name of the newspaper and date are visible. At the top of the page, I add the title "GUILTY" as large as I can above it. Fifty copies should be enough.

I pull on my coat; the envelope finds a home in my inside pocket. The stack of fliers rest along my arm. I try to tell the voice inside my head that tonight is not the right time to deliver such a message. It won't listen.

The same voice in my head leads me to my car and guides me along the roads to Woodhaven.

To Olivia's house.

Chapter Twenty

Olivia

I stop people on the streets of Woodhaven, hoping to find Calvin's friend. They either ignore me, spit at me, or tell me to "get the fuck out of town." I stand on the corner south of my bookstore, defeated. I need to find this mystery person. They are the key to all of this.

I was hoping to find Mrs. Olson at her usual bench with the other women who preach to me about my sins. She knows everything that goes on in this town and would know about any mystery people Calvin spent time with. I'll try to find her at her house. I regret I didn't start there. Perhaps, I could have avoided all this harassment.

I turn back towards my car and SMACK! My shoulder collides with something hard. I rub the point of impact to ease the pain. "Sorry I..."

Ernest Taylor, Shaylynn's father, stands before me. He's unkempt with wrinkled clothes he's worn for days. His red, swollen eyes enlarge when they land on me. The wafts of cigarette smoke are strong.

"YOU!"

"Ernest, I'm sor-"

"You don't get to speak. Your son killed my little girl, and you didn't stop him. What type of mother can't control their own son, huh? And now, you walk around town like nothing happened. I hope you both rot in hell!" He shoves me off-balance and into the street.

His disappointment that I'm not hit by a car is evident. I don't blame him. I would hope for the same thing, if I were him. He continues down the street, looking back over his shoulder twice, before going into the pharmacy.

I pull myself together and head to Mrs. Olson's. Even if she hates me, she will try to gather as much information from me as she can. I will do the same with her.

Mrs. Olson's brownstone blends into the line of row houses that cover the entire block. The same white brick encases every building, all stained with years of dust carried on the wind from the forest. Her blue door causes her house to stand out from the rest.

Mrs. Olson emerges from her door before I even open her front gate. "I was wondering when you were going to come see me." Her grin gives me goosebumps. She waves me inside. "Let me take your coat."

"Thank you." She puts it on an iron hook beside the door.

"I put on some tea before you arrived. Head into the drawing room and I will bring it out." The living room is tiny, not a receiving area for royalty, but Mrs. Olson likes to put on airs, and now is not the time to call her out.

As quick as she's gone, the tea is in my hands.

"Now, my sweet girl, how can I help?" Her kindness cuts like a dagger.

"Have you ever seen Calvin spend time with someone other than Shaylynn?"

"Hmm." She sips her tea, as she savours my unease. "Not that I can recall, and you know my recall is the best in town."

"I do, and that is why I'm hoping you might remember someone. Not a regular around town. Perhaps an outsider?"

"Plenty of people pass through, many of whom visit your bookstore. How is business, by the way?"

Oh, how I want to slap the smirk off her face, "As you are aware, the business is temporarily closed while I support Calvin."

"I saw the wood panels covering the store windows. Shame what happened."

"When people act out irrationally, things get broken. But it's just glass. I will fix it when all this is over."

"Oh, darling, you don't think the town will let you stay here, do you?"

As much as I want information, I can't handle her backhanded kindness. "You uptight, self-righteous bitch! Yes, I said it. You think you're better than everyone else and that you know what happened to Shaylynn. Well, my son is innocent and I'll prove it. I was hoping you could help, but I see you will not get off your high horse and use your snooping skills to do anything more than gossip. I'll just find this mystery person by myself. Oh, and your tea tastes horrible!"

Dismayed, it takes Mrs. Olson a moment to catch up to me in her garden. "The sooner you admit the truth, the sooner you can get on with your life. There's no mystery person, Olivia. I would have noticed."

"Just like you noticed your husband having an affair for three years?" I wasn't holding back my punches.

"You little... I hope you and that devil son of yours rot in hell."

"I'm getting that a lot today. Thanks to you, and the rest of this town, I'm already in it."

Mrs. Olson slams her door, and the front window vibrates. I pull the gate so hard the handle comes off in my hands. I shove it in my coat pocket. She can find another one.

Outraged, I don't notice I'm driving double the speed limit. My tires squeal as I turn into my driveway and gravel pelts the undercarriage and sides of my car. I scream into the void of my car as loud as I can. Everything's falling apart. I'm useless and my son will go to jail for the rest of his life if I don't do something. I need a very large drink.

John waltzes out of my house. "Did you decide to ditch the bookstore and become a race car driver?"

"Now is not the time for jokes. I need wine." I brush past him.

"Okay, well, I stocked up, so pick your poison."

Why was he being so nice? Couldn't he do or say something that would let me yell at him? A fight would stop me from focusing on my failures.

Glassware collides with my counter top. I release a cork from the grip of a bottle and liquid pours.

John sits beside me on the couch. "Did the visit with Calvin go well?"

"Horrible. He barely looked at me and wouldn't let me explain why I kept his father a secret. I wasn't able to speak to him at all. He kicked me out of the room when the subject of some mystery friend came up."

"Friend?"

"Yeah, some no-named person Calvin met that Mr. Bower is trying to find. They might have knowledge to help us, but no one knows who they are."

"But everyone knows everybody in this town."

"Exactly, but Calvin won't let Mr. Bower tell me anything, so I'm grasping at straws trying to find this person and there are no leads to go on."

"Mrs. Olson might-"

"I just came from there and, well, that was a shit show and now I own a souvenir, the handle to her gate."

"I'm sorry, the handle to her gate?"

"Apparently, I have super strength." I toss the handle onto the table. "Now I just need to break Calvin out of prison, as I'm not sure I'm getting him out of there any other way." I gulp down my wine and pour another.

"We'll figure-"

"This out? Bullshit. The evidence is solid. If I were investigating, I would assume Calvin was guilty. Maybe I do?"

"Stop. Unless he became possessed, Calvin didn't do this."

"So now it's not whatever God has planned, but my son's possessed by the Devil. You are clutching at anything for an explanation. We're so fucked."

"That's not what I meant, but sure. Let's go with the Devil and yes, a third glass of wine in five minutes seems like an acceptable intake of alcohol. Why don't-"

SLAP!

My hand finds the side of John's face before I can stop myself. Stunned silence surrounds us.

Afraid I might hit him again, I bolt to the arched doorway between the living room and dining room. "I'm so sorry. I don't know why I did that."

John presses his hand to his cheek to ease the sting. "I'm sorry I commented on your drinking. You've had a stressful day."

"That's no excuse." I was looking for a verbal fight, not a physical one.

"It's okay. I'm fine. I won't even bruise. Let's turn our attention elsewhere. You got this letter today."

"Great, hate mail. What I've always wanted."

"It could be helpful?"

"You open it. I've had enough verbal beatings from townies today, no point in taking a written one as well."

John tears open the sealed envelope, unfolds the letter, and stops. His eyes dart around the room, avoiding my gaze and his jaw clenches.

"What horrible things are people saying now?"

"I don't want to show this to you, but you need to see it." His voice cracks. "You should sit."

This is the second time John has asked me to sit before he'll tell me something. I hesitate, but he looks devastated, so I retake my place on the couch. The photos are in my possession for milliseconds before my wine glass shatters on the floor.

CHAPTER TWENTY-ONE

STRANGER

Olivia's screams reach the hedge I hide behind. The left side of my mouth turns upwards. Revenge is better than any whiskey I've tasted.

My binoculars follow Olivia's every movement. She crumples up the letter and tries, with all her strength, to throw it across the room. It flies but a few inches. She tosses the gifted photos in the air like confetti. Except Olivia isn't celebrating.

Olivia turns her anger towards anything within reach. The wine bottle smashes against the wall and creates red splatter art that resembles a large pool of blood trickling down the wallpaper. She flips the coffee table and a chair almost flies through the front window. Reverend John steps in just in time, and eases the chair back onto the floor, Olivia's hands gripped around the chair's arms.

Until that moment, Reverend John had remained seated on the couch, observing the monster unleash itself. Disaster is left in its wake. All the work they did to clean up after the Woodhaven police searched her home has been erased.

Reverend John tries to guide Olivia to sit down. The torment is too much, she refuses, and further screams filter into the evening air.

With the contents of one envelope, I have taken away all hope Olivia had. Agony conducts a symphony of beauty. The words I'd written scroll before my eyes.

I know who you are. Olivia Sophia Beaumont.

If you think hard enough, you'll know the person behind this piece of paper. The time we spent together was brief, but the impact you had on my family was monumental.

Do you remember that day on the train, after you killed William? How nervous you were when the gentlemen sat across from you and took his time unwinding his scarf from his face? I doubt anyone else noticed your hands shaking, but I did. Were you worried you hadn't taken back your freedom? That someone you feared had found you?

Not only had I found you. I've followed you for the past eighteen years. Waiting. See any brown trench coats walking around town? You almost saw me on the train. However, I anticipated your move before it happened and left the train car.

You've been so distracted you didn't even see me when you walked right into me outside the police station after Calvin's arrest. I'm surprised you didn't recognize me. Given how close we had gotten at Hammond Manor.

These photos are only a glimpse into what your son has become. Does he remind you of anyone?

I flip through the photographs in my mind.

Photo 1: Shaylynn is running, her auburn hair flying around her. A terrified look is on her face. A male with light brown hair chases her.

Photo 2: The male, now identifiably Calvin, grips both of Shaylynn's arms. He is yelling at her. Shaylynn looks right into the camera, pleading for help.

Photo 3: Calvin is running after Shaylynn again. This time with a knife in his left hand.

Photo 4: Calvin stands over Shaylynn's body. Knife dripping with blood. His face is expressionless.

An ominous silence draws my attention to the house. The lights are still on, but where are Olivia or Reverend John?

They're leaving.

Dirt jams under my nails as I scramble to hide around the side of the hedge. Their headlights catch the toes of my boot as I dash out of sight.

I catch my breath once the car is down the hill and no longer in view. The last lines of my letter play in my head.

I told you I would get revenge for my sister.
Dr. M. Harrison

CHAPTER TWENTY-TWO

OLIVIA

I am becoming too familiar with the Woodhaven police station. The smell of stale coffee and disingenuous comments of concern fill the air. I don't wait to be directed to DI Whitaker's desk. I run past an officer as they exit the secure area. The Constable on the front desk yells after me.

I find DI Whitaker and Officer Cole staring at a wall of photos and papers. "Ma'am, you can't be here!" The Constable yells behind me. John trails him.

DI Whitaker whirls around. "It's okay Dan. We'll take her into the conference room."

"Now, Ms. Lyons. Or should I say Beaumont? Want to tell me what has gotten you all fired up tonight?"

"How do you know my name? Nevermind. My son is being set up. He didn't kill Shaylynn!"

"Is that so? Our evidence points to the contrary, and you remember how evidence works, right? Now, I know how you like your wine. How much have you had tonight?"

"That has nothing to do with this. Someone dropped this off and it proves someone else is involved." Have they turned the temperature up in the conference room or is it just me?

John stands silent against the glass wall separating the room from the hallway. Officer Cole positions herself in the doorway and observes, straight-faced.

DI Whitaker reads the note, sighs, and the side of his mouth twitches. "This crumpled letter means nothing. I know this is hard for you but, you're drunk and desperate to find anything to help your son. You likely wrote this yourself."

"The fuck I did!" I was toe to toe with DI Whitaker. My fists were balled up and ready to throw a punch if another condescending word came out of his mouth.

John pulls me back. "Now, Daniel. Let's play nice. I found the letter, not Olivia."

"That doesn't mean she didn't leave it for you to find."

"And where would she have printed it? You took her printer and no one in town will help her. I can barely wash the graffiti off her house before more appears."

"I don't suppose the bookstore has a printer, now does it? By the way, a search warrant to search the place is pending. Should receive it in a couple of days. Anyway, the shape this letter is in, I won't be able to get anything off it. Maybe if you hadn't lost your temper, I could have gotten prints off it."

I squeeze the back of a chair and clench my teeth. "Detective, can you read? The name Dr. M. Harrison is very visible."

"Ah yes, the mysterious doctor who performed a C-section on you and left you to die. Officer Cole, were you able to find anything on this M. Harrison?"

"Nothing sir. No one alive in the United Kingdom matches the description."

"People change over the years," I say.

"Well, yes, but as far as we can tell, the one you are talking about is dead." DI Whitaker said.

"That can't be. Why would anyone else sign her name?"

"I don't know, Olivia, why would they?" DI Whitaker asks.

I want to show him the accompanying photos someone else took that night. However, that would only make things worse for Calvin. "I didn't write this letter. God, you people are idiots."

"That's enough. We're done here. John, take her home. Try to keep her there and maybe hide the alcohol." He doesn't wait for a response and stomps past Officer Cole. She nods and follows him.

"I can't believe this. He's ignoring what is right in front of his face."

"Liv, let's talk about this back at your place. Charlotte should arrive soon."

Was it the weekend already? Little sleep blended all the days together.

If these people can't find out what happened to Dr. Harrison, Charlotte will.

I cry when I see the woman with the round face and hazel eyes sitting on my front step. I wrap my arms around her, and my tears soak her shoulder. Charlotte will restore my hope.

Once my arms are too tired to hold her anyone, the three of us gather in the disaster that is my living room.

"What happened here?" Charlotte asks.

"I did," I say.

"Gotcha. Then you need a drink."

I glare at John to prevent any further comments on my drinking. "Well, I know I could use one," he says.

Charlotte pulls out a bottle of vodka from one of her bags and heads into the dining room. The furniture is still upright and usable. Two shots each and we get to work. I reiterate everything I told Charlotte on the phone yesterday and update her on the horrifying revelation of today.

"Wait, Doctor Harrison is alive? We searched for her for months and came up empty. A few years ago, one of our algorithms caught a hit on a death announcement in the Portree Herald, a small town in Scotland. I thought she was dead."

"DI Whitaker thinks the same thing. But he can't see past Calvin. He doesn't know what the Hammonds are like. The lengths they will go to. You believe me though, right?"

"Of course. You don't have to keep asking me that. Dr. Harrison would be smart enough to fake her own death. She'd be what? Eight-two now. The obituary states she, or someone with that name, died of a heart attack. If that's the case, no one would question anything. It's possible she is dead and someone

95

is using her name to distract you. Just in case, let's make a list of anyone you know who would want to hurt you. The Doctor herself, who else?"

For twenty-minutes we document any Hammond, their staff, and high-profile guests who visited Hammond Manor.

"What about Caldwell?" I ask. "He took pleasure in my pain and would do anything for Helen. I still swear they were hiding a relationship."

"All the alerts we have set up on him haven't had a hit. It's as if he disappeared. He must have had other identities set up just like Helen and William."

The hairs on my neck stand up. "So he could be involved?"

"Possible, but my gut tells me he would have acted by now. He doesn't have Helen to keep him on a leash, and I'm sure he would have lashed out at you if he was close by."

"Maybe. Have we missed anyone?"

As if reading my mind, John speaks up, "You should add me to that list."

Charlotte stares at him.

"It isn't me, but neither of you will be satisfied until you rule me out. So you better include me."

Charlotte runs over to John and wraps her arms around him. "This is why I love you. No one in their right mind would offer themself up."

John has an annoying habit of cracking his knuckles when he's nervous. He's been doing it for the last ten minutes.

"Please stop. The bone cracking is aggravating." I say.

"Sorry." He cups one hand around the other, on top of the table, and taps his fingers on the back of the opposite hand.

Charlotte kisses his cheek and adds, "it also helps that I could corroborate your story about when you found out who your parents were. There were only three printings of your birth certificate. One when you were born, one four years ago; as you said, and one a month ago."

"Who requested it a month ago?" John asks.

"It said John, but the application was electronic and the IP address doesn't match John's home network or the cell phone towers in this area."

"You know my IP address?"

"I know a lot of things" Charlotte winks and nods towards me.

John brushes his hands through his hair, gets up from the table and gazes out the living room window. "Good news. No pitch forks yet."

"Oh, I bet they're just sharpening them." Vodka coats my throat. "And I'm sorry I doubted you."

"I've already forgiven you for that, remember? Now, let's focus on who might be after you."

Folders emerge from one of Charlotte's suitcases. "What I'm about to show both of you is confidential. I would lose my job if anyone ever found out I allowed you to look at these. John, please close the curtains. We don't need any nosy neighbours watching us."

The Woodhaven Police insignia covers the front of the folders. "Where? How? You know what? I should know better than to ask." I smile.

"Yes, you should. Let's see if anything points to Doctor Harrison being involved and where she might be."

We sift through the information twice. It all points to Calvin.

"It's no use. There's nothing here." I say.

"What about this?" John says.

"What?"

"Isn't Calvin right handed?"

"Yes."

"Then why is the bloody knife in his left hand? I've never stabbed anyone, but I would think I would use my dominant hand. Am I wrong?"

I rip the photo from John's hand. I grab the other photo of Calvin holding the knife. "In this one, before there's blood on the knife, it's in his right hand." I look closer at the photos. "Could someone have altered these?"

Charlotte takes the photos and squints, "Nothing's impossible, but these would be really well done. Let's run the scenario before I call my tech guys to look into this."

I pace around the dining room table. "Let's say the photos have been altered. Then maybe the knife was never in Calvin's hand when it entered Shaylynn. Where's the photo of the knife with Calvin's bloody fingerprints?"

"Here." We gather around the photo Charlotte holds out. "Does this not look a little too perfect? All of Calvin's prints are in the blood." I say.

Charlotte continues my thought, "As though the blood was there before the prints."

"Exactly. My prints at the top of the handle make sense. After I cleaned it, my fingerprints would remain when I put it in the butcher block. If the killer added blood to the knife after Shaylynn was stabbed, it may not have covered my print on the top edge. If they wrapped Calvin's hand around the knife, once the blood was on it, this would explain how the unique grooves of Calvin's prints are clearly visible."

Charlotte joins me on a circular trip around the dining room table. The photo is in the center. "We know whoever is playing this twisted game with you was in the forest that night because someone took photos of Calvin and Shaylynn. What if they subdued Calvin somehow and went after Shaylynn? Calvin wakes up beside her, covered in her blood and no memory of what happened. Doctored photos might be enough to create reasonable doubt. If not, it's a start."

"Another question," John says, "why is this print on the tip of the blade not labeled like the rest?"

How was he picking up on what Charlotte and I hadn't seen? "Maybe you should turn in your collar for a badge." John chuckles at my joke. Another review of the photo reveals it's a partial print.

Charlotte pulls out the report that accompanies the photo. "It said it was unidentifiable, but not a match to yours or Calvin's."

Hope grows inside me. "That's it! It has to be Doctor Harrison's. Please tell me she didn't have her prints seared off like the rest of the goddamn Hammond family."

"Only one way to find out. I'm going to make some calls. Olivia, maybe you should call Ray Bower and see when he can meet with us. Hopefully, my team has answered our questions by then. Or at least, we can point him in a direction to look further."

We make some more calls and consume more vodka. The liquor cannot silence the voice in the back of my mind. *What you're finding doesn't matter. Calvin still could have killed Shaylynn. The Hammonds have a way of forcing people to do unexpected things.*

CHAPTER TWENTY-THREE

CALVIN

The meeting room is unchanged. Sterile furniture and floors reflect the fluorescent lights from above. "What do you mean there are photos?" I ask Mr. Bower. Warmth envelopes me and my sweat makes me itchy.

Mr. Bower's suit shows no sign of a wrinkle and his face so no sign of concern over this new revelation.

"Posters like this went up all over Woodhaven. And the police received an anonymous package with these photos in it." Mr. Bower scatters everything on the table.

The hairs on my neck stand tall. My stomach lurches like I'm on a roller-coaster. Are my eyes lying to me? A photo of me towering over Shaylynn's lifeless body with a knife.

I can't deny it anymore. The voice in my head has been right all along. I am my father.

"Who was with you that night?" Mr. Bower asks.

"No one."

"Someone took these photos. Shaylynn is looking right at them. So who was there?"

I stare at the pictures. Whoever took them stood behind me. From the angle of the photo, they could have been up against my back. Memories stay hidden inside of me. "I don't remember."

"Look, kid, with these, all I can probably do for you is try to get you a reduced sentence. But we need to give the crown prosecutor something as a bargaining chip. I go in there now and it's life, without parole. Period."

"How many times do I have to tell you I don't remember?" Why does no one believe me?

"We're running out of time. Your appointment with the therapist is in a few hours. In the meantime, don't talk to anyone. We don't need someone in here using whatever you say against you."

I drop my head to the table. It's cold metal filters through my forehead and down my body. The heat emitting from me turns down a couple of degrees.

"I'll be back soon. We're going to try and figure out who the photographer is."

I hear the door behind me open. A hand on my arm pulls me off the table. My surroundings blur and my feet move without instruction. I'm focusing on one thing.

I killed my best friend.

"Holy shit, he looks like a ghost," an inmate whispers.

"Hey newbie, have a visit with the Superintendent? Not someone you want to piss off." another inmate says. Laughter ripples from the group around a common-area table. The noise of the crowd pulls my thoughts to what's happening around me. The voice inside my head falls away in the distance.

"He probably found out he's never leaving. Murderers don't get out now, do they, newbie?" a large bald man covered in tattoos says.

I step towards the voice, fists at my side. If he wants to fight, I'd be more than happy to use his face to release my pent-up anger. The guard comes between me and the group, grips my arm, and ushers me to my cell. "Probably best to stay here."

"Why do you care what happens to me?"

"Given what happened in the cafeteria, and the reason you're in here, you could cause a lot of harm. So stay where I can see you."

"Oh, I have a babysitter now."

"The words you are looking for are, thank you for your help, Marc. I appreciate you looking out for me so that I don't get my ass kicked and get in more trouble." He turns and steps sideways. I don't have to see him to know he hasn't gone far.

So this would be the next seventy years of my life? Ushered around a prison like a rat in a maze. Only to find myself in a tiny room with little else but my thoughts. I can't do this for the rest of my life. It's only been a few days, and it is becoming too much.

Lying on the bed, my ankles kiss the edge of the bed frame. Tears well up and I hug the paper-thin pillow over my face to hide them.

"I'm so sorry, Shaylynn," I think. "I wanted none of this. Wherever you are, I hope you believe me. I'd do anything to have you back. I miss your laugh and the way you always stole my last chip. You never tried to be sneaky about it. You'd stare at me, smile and take it."

"I want to turn back time and find a dingy flat in London. Like that one you found online, with the smallest bathroom in the world but a brilliant view of the gardens across the street. I want us to dance all night at the best clubs. Even if my footwork needs, well, work. I want us to meet interesting people and live our lives the way we want to. Together."

"Because of me, we can't."

"There's proof that I took away those moments from us. From you."

"For two years, confusion about who I am took over. You tried to help me figure out who I would become after learning about my actual family. Now, I guess I know."

"I'm William Hammond Jr., with a different name."

CHAPTER TWENTY-FOUR

CALVIN

The examination table in the middle of the prison doctor's office is uncomfortable. The coarse paper crinkles with the slightest movement. Unlike my cell, the room is well lit, with natural light unimpeded by bars on the windows.

The therapist, whose name I have already forgotten, is young. She probably doesn't know what she is doing. What a waste of time.

"If you were present at an event, then it's buried in your brain somewhere. It might take time, but we'll find it. For hypnosis to work I will need you to do exactly as I say. Unclench your hands and rest them beside you. Good. Now let's start by closing your eyes and picturing your bedroom. Can you see it?" the therapist asks.

"This is ridiculous. Can I please leave?" I ask.

Mr. Bower doesn't look impressed. "Calvin, just listen to her. She's trying to help you."

Everyone's trying to help me, but no one actually is. "Fine. My bedroom."

"Tell me about it," the therapist says.

"Um. There's a dresser to the left of the door. My bed is in the far corner. Beside it is a desk, under the window, and then a closet to the right of the desk"

"Focus on the top of the dresser. Tell me everything that sits on it."

"Three football trophies, some candy wrappers, deodorant containers, and a black sock."

"Now, I want you to picture the beach of Woodhaven Bay. Tell me about that."

"The sand is soft by the water, but a little rough further up the shore. Small stones of different colours litter the beach. Waves crash into the sand and go from blue to white. The water goes out over the horizon and beyond. Boats float in the distance."

The clicking clock, Mr. Bower's tapping foot, and the noise from the hallway filters away.

"Let's go back to the night in the forest. What's happening?"

"Shaylynn's beside me and we step onto the boardwalk. We walk to the end, lean against the wooden rail and stare out at the ocean. She says something, but I can't hear it. Smiling, she climbs onto the rail and stands with her arms spread open. The breeze causes each strand to fly behind her. She hollers. Or at least her mouth opens wide. I can only hear the water in the bay."

"I help her down from the rail and she tries to get me to stand on it. Afraid of water, I refuse. I'm not sure where the fear comes from. Probably, my mom, as she's always been afraid of drowning."

"Shaylynn walks back towards the shore. I run and catch up with her. We're getting closer to the forest. No one else is around. We break the tree line and play tag between the trees like we are children. I let her catch me, so that I can feel her hands on me."

"Shaylynn stops in her tracks. There's a white flash. She looks back at me. Her cobalt blue eyes are full of concern. I step beside her. Another flash. Shaylynn squeezes my hand."

"Someone is coming towards us. Someone dressed in all black. They have a knife. They run towards us."

"We turn and run. White flash. I grip Shaylynn's hand with all my strength. She leads the way and looks back. White flash. She trips and falls. I land on top of her."

"We scramble to our feet and I look back. The dark figure is gone. The sound of waves is replaced by rapid heartbeats."

"We run through the forest towards town, the way we were heading before the black figure appeared. It's the quickest way home. The moonlight brightens the small opening in the middle of the forest. We step into it. So does..."

"Calvin, who do you see?" the therapist asks.

"I don't know. There's no face. They are a dark blur."

"Shaylynn runs over to them, her mouth moving quickly. There's still no sound. Shaylynn wraps her arms around the blurry person. The person guides Shaylynn back to me."

"Something silver flashes in the moonlight. I can't see what it is. It's gone."

"My eyelids are heavy. The trees become hazy. Shaylynn falls to the ground. My legs are weak. Then. Darkness."

A squeeze of my hand brings me back to the doctor's office.

"That's great. You can open your eyes."

"Are we done?"

"For today."

"No, I need to understand what happened. Who that other person was. Let's keep going?"

"You're drenched in sweat and cold to the touch. Your body needs to rest."

"I don't want to rest. I want to know how I killed my friend."

"These things take time and we need to be-"

"Time! I don't have time. Now help me or I'm going-"

Mr. Bower pushes my chest back against the examination table. "I know it's not what you want, but we'll stop for today. We want to ensure what you recall are clear memories, not ones distorted from exhaustion and anxiety. We'll sort this out, but you need to trust the process."

"The process sucks."

"There's nothing stopping you from trying to remember outside of these sessions. Just don't force it too hard. If I'm going to help you, we need to trust your memories. We'll be back tomorrow."

Forest scenes project onto the corridor walls on my way back to my cell. Shaylynn falls, but she isn't hurt. I don't have a knife when darkness takes over. What happened between then and when I woke up beside her dead body?

My hand tingles as it grips an invisible knife.

CHAPTER TWENTY-FIVE

CALVIN

I take my spot on the examination table. This time there's no crinkle paper. Less distraction, the therapist says. A single ray of sunlight muddles through the grey clouds outside and shines on the linoleum floor. The scent of alcohol from the sanitizer lingers in the air.

Mr. Bower assures me today we will find the answers. I just need to push a little harder. Go a little further back in my memory.

The therapist sits beside me. Her knees touch the side of the table. Her voice comes out just above a whisper, "Calvin, you did great yesterday. We'll do the same thing again today. Starting with focusing on your bedroom, then the beach and then try to go to the incident right before everything goes dark."

I go through the exercise. The sound of waves once again pulls me into the forest.

"Shaylynn hits the ground beside me. Her hair falls over her face. The moonlight shines on her like she is the only one in the forest. My legs are weak. My chest is warm and tight. The person stands between Shaylynn and I – they are still a blurry blob. I'm lowered to the ground. I can't move."

"Leaves rustle beside me. My head is as heavy as a ten-pin bowling ball. I want to look around but a force fights back. It takes all my strength to turn my head to the right. Shaylynn is now lying on her back, hands at her sides. Someone

105

brushed the hair that covered her face behind her ears. Her chest moves up and down."

"I haven't killed her yet. Darkness."

"There's a narrow beam of light. Something is coming into focus. Shaylynn is running away from me. I'm holding a knife. It's clean. We run through the trees and I tell her I won't hurt her, but she keeps running."

"She looks different. Her hair has turned into snakes. They slither around her head. She stumbles on a fallen tree. She looks up at me. Her eyes are hollow, black. She's turned into some sort of monster. I need to save her. I need to kill the monster. Moonlight kisses the blade as it rises above me. Shaylynn lurches forward after the first impact. She claws at me. I slap her hand away. I watch blood ooze out around the knife's blade. Half the knife sticks out from Shaylynn's stomach."

"The blackness of her eyes is spreading to her face. The monster isn't dead. Why won't it die? I pull the knife out, ready to attack again, but the sight of all the blood makes me nauseous."

"I roll off her body and run to a tree. I vomit. A hand grabs my shoulder. Darkness."

A squeeze of my hand brings me out of hypnosis.

"That's good, Calvin," the therapist says. "We'll try again tomorrow."

"No. Now. Put me back under now."

"All of this is very traumatic. The more we push, the worse off you could be."

"Worse than being in jail for murder? Please do your voodoo thing again."

She looks to Mr. Bower, who nods, and we go again.

"There's a sharp pain in the back of my head. My heart wants to jump out of my chest. The tips of my fingers are chilled. I crush twigs and leaves crackle under my hands as I slowly push myself to a seated position. The dark forest around me spins."

"I turn my head. Shaylynn is ghost white. Dead. No! No! No!"

"Calvin, that's enough." The therapist and Mr. Bower try to hold down my flailing arms.

"Again, we have to go again. I need to go back to when the hand grabs my shoulder."

The therapist tries to be calm, but frustration filters from her voice. "It's possible you can't go back there. Your brain may have blocked out those memories completely."

"You said, if it happened, it's in my head. Let's go again."

Mr. Bower speaks up. "Calvin, stop. You remember stabbing Shaylynn once. Is that not enough?"

"Please. I just need to know everything."

"Maybe it's better if you don't," he says.

I let my body go limp. No longer having to fight me, Mr. Bower and the therapist step back. They talk in a corner and I focus on the speckled ceiling above.

What if Mr. Bower's right? Did I really want to watch myself stab Shaylynn more than once? Once made me a murderer.

Chapter Twenty-Six

Stranger

I hide the gaps of dark blue and gold wallpaper with my fresh additions. The Guardian, The Telegraph, and especially the Woodhaven Times run daily coverage of Shaylynn's murder. With the revelation of who Olivia is, reporters are feeding on the development. Her past is strewn over the newspapers' pages. Helen would be proud.

The trial starts in a few days, and all eyes are on Calvin. My contacts within the police department assure me there are no holes in their case. Which means there were no holes in my plan. I need to continue to evade Charlotte and MI5.

Once the trial is over, I will seek revenge against Charlotte. It's not only Olivia who will feel my wrath. Charlotte will stand by, and feel helpless, as her best friend loses everything, while she can do nothing. She will feel as I did when Helen had to flee, when she got arrested and when the other prisoners beat her to death in the shower. My heart shatters to a hundred pieces, wishing I had protected her.

Once Olivia has lost everything, so will Charlotte, and together they will die. Then my full plan will come to fruition.

The sun spotlights an article on my wall about Reverend John's community work with the homeless. When the Reverend puts his mind to something, he follows it through and gets significant results. It's a pity Woodhaven has turned on him like Olivia. Attendance at Sunday Mass was dismal – six people.

KNOCK, KNOCK.

I draw the floor-to-ceiling curtain along the wall to hide my compilation. The gun, from the table beside the front door, rests in my hand.

Relief overtakes me when I peer through the peephole. The unexpected man stands hunched inside his jacket, trying his best to hide from the rain. His unmistakable eyes peer above his collar.

I tuck the gun back in its home and open the door. It only opens a crack before he barges in, shaking like a wet dog. Pellets of water slap my face.

"We have a problem," Buck says.

"What is it?"

"I don't know how much longer I can distract people from looking for you. He's recalling what happened." His eyes dart around the sitting room, stopping on the curtain, before resting on me.

"How is he remembering? The drug should have erased all memories."

"Nothing's perfect. I told you that. He's working with this therapist and her skills are better than I would expect."

"I thought someone straight out of school was his therapist?"

"She is."

"Then how is she helping him?"

"I don't understand all this crap. It only took a few drinks at the pub by the prison, before she mentioned the possibility of other people being present that night. She didn't say who, but if word gets out-"

"End the sessions and handle this. Handle her."

"Isn't that taking it too far? We already have enough blood on our hands."

"There is never enough blood on our hands when it comes to protecting family. Eighteen years, I've waited for this moment, and some therapist will not get in my way. Do you understand me? If you can't handle it, I will."

"Don't you think it'll be suspicious, the boy's therapist dying as he's remembering what happened?"

"No one needs to find out he's remembering, now do they? Make her death appear to be an accident. Do I have to walk you through the process of how to do that, or do you think you can handle that one task on your own?"

"I'll take care of it, but we need to be careful or everything will unravel. Your note hasn't helped."

"On the contrary, it has. Olivia and her friends are scrambling and not paying attention to what is happening right in front of them. I've been to her house twice since this all started and not a soul in or out of the building has noticed." The comfort of my Wingback chair eases the bout of stress. "Make me some tea."

We sit in silence for a while and listen to the rain. The plan will still be successful. The therapist is a bump in the road, but Buck will remove it. He's had to make something appear to be an accident before. Six years ago, he was driving home and was distracted by an article on his phone and killed an old man on a bicycle. Buck put the man and his bike in his trunk and drove him home. Living in a small town, he knew the old man lived alone and set up the scene to look like he'd fallen out of the shower and hit his head on the toilet.

Buck dismantled the bike, took a boat out into the English Channel late one night, and tossed it overboard. The police never suspected foul play.

"How did your talk go today?" I ask.

"Low attendance again, and I'm sure I put them all to sleep. No one wants to hear what I say. They feel obligated to attend, so it's an opportunity for an hour-long nap."

"Nonsense. I'm sure someone got something out of your words. Keep at it, and your audience will become more engaged and grow."

"Time is not something I have a lot of left."

"The Doctor didn't share good news?"

"The cancer continues to spread and chemo isn't working. I don't know how much I want to fight this devil anymore. I might let it take me."

Buck's treatment has not reduced his size, but he is frail in other ways. His temper gets the better of him more often than not, and he is becoming less enthusiastic about our plan. Some days I don't recognize an ounce of Hammond in him. The more he pulls away from his family obligations, the more the reality of having to tie up a loose end becomes clearer.

I push away the thought. As calculating as I can be, I am not sure I can take the life of my son

CHAPTER TWENTY-SEVEN

OLIVIA

The results of Charlotte's calls come in throughout the day. However, she wants to wait until everyone's at the house before she shares the information. I'm not sure if that means there isn't much to discuss, or if she's trying to protect me until she has reinforcements to handle my reaction.

I force John to leave and pick us up something to eat for dinner. He fights me on it, but he needs a break. Even if it's only thirty minutes.

Ray Bower's on his way to my house and, together, the four of us are going to figure this whole mess out. I'm confident we are smart enough to take on Doctor Harrison. But can we do it before the trial?

I'd do anything to stop Calvin from having to go through the horrible process of the British judicial system. All the press and accusations. Hell, I don't want to go through it. Again.

The hinges of my front door creak, and the aroma of fried chicken fills the house. A familiar comfort.

"Look who pulled up behind me," John says. Ray squeezes into the narrow hallway beside John.

"How is Calvin doing?" I ask.

"Let him get his jacket off," John says.

"Sorry."

"It's alright. He's okay. We've been working with a helpful therapist." Ray replies.

"Has he remembered anything?"

"Well, yes. But it's hard to decipher what is real, and what is fantasy."

"What do you mean?" John asks, littering the few empty spaces on the dining room table with food containers.

"Well, he remembers Shaylynn turning into some sort of monster with no eyes and snakes for hair."

"Was he on any drugs that night?" I ask.

Charlotte looks over some records. "Toxicology report came back, and he had a bit of alcohol in his system, nothing to the extent to make him see things. No drugs."

"Could my son seeing a monster help him? Could he have some sort of reduced capacity defense?"

"I'm not the therapist, so I can't tell you the significance of the monster. I can tell you, if one memory from those sessions gets entered as evidence, they all do. We can't pick what the judge learns. And there is a memory you don't want revealed."

The chicken leg in my hand shakes. "What is that?"

"He remembers stabbing Shaylynn."

The chicken hits my plate and sauce splatters all over me. "He...but...no." My worst nightmare is coming true. Calvin is his father.

John pulls his chair towards mine until the two touch. He wraps his arms around me. "He vividly remembers this?" he asks.

"It was a pretty clear memory. He said he was on top of her, after she fell, and then he stabbed her."

John squeezes my hand and despite his arms around me, cold envelopes me. I've lost my voice.

"What did he say about who took the pictures?" Charlotte asks.

"Might have been someone dressed head-to-toe in black. But Calvin believes, they ran off before anything bad happened. That being said, he later recalls what he thinks is a person, but his memory has blurred them out. He doesn't know who that person is."

I can't breathe, and am thankful Charlotte and John are asking the questions.

"So this mystery person could have taken the photos of Calvin with the knife?" Charlotte asks.

"Possibly. He doesn't fully recall the events. His memories jump all over the place but they mostly focus before the death and then when he wakes up beside her"

"But you'll keep trying, right?" John asks.

"As long as it's not harmful to Calvin, yes."

John rests his head against mine and whispers, "How can I help?"

My vocal chords struggle to move. I finally squeeze out, "I need air."

My chair topples to the ground behind me. I can't get out of my house fast enough. The cool, sea salt air slaps my skin. He killed her. My baby killed her. My knees buckle. The cold, lush grass softens my fall. I punch the ground in front of me, but the tension, hurt, and confusion don't subside.

This is all my fault. I shouldn't have brought him here. I should have refused Charlotte's offer and gotten as far away from this country as possible. But no, I wanted to be close enough to the one person I could trust. But look what good that did. Even Charlotte, with all her tracing, tracking, and alerts, couldn't prevent what was happening.

I lie back on the grass and watch pillows of clouds float along the summer's evening sky. Birds frolic and sing underneath them. No sign of sunset in sight. Would I ever feel the happiness I had when Calvin and I didn't have a care in the world? Or were those moments now lost in the sea of terrible memories?

The gnomes in my garden watch me. Their beady eyes and tiny smirks are creepy. Calvin carefully picked each one, so now they live in our flower beds. All-seeing.

A growing shadow casts itself upon me.

"I brought you this." I sit up and John wraps a blanket around me. Despite the summer heat, I grasp the blanket for warmth and security. "Anything else I can get you?"

"Can you sit with me? We need to go over what Charlotte found out, but for a few minutes, I don't want to talk about my imploding world."

"What do you want to talk about?"

"Um. How did your sermon go today?"

"How well does it go every Sunday? It's a good time for a nap."

"You don't give yourself enough credit."

"It's hard to be passionate when a handful of people show up, and only so they can lecture me after my sermon."

"I'm sorry this is happening to you."

"It's not your fault. Don't look at me like that. It's not. Besides, I've been considering retiring."

"Give up the luxurious Reverend life. How will you cope?"

"I love that even though you're heartbroken and lost, your wit never leaves you."

"It's a defense mechanism. Pick another topic and let's see what I can come up with."

"I went to my doctor today."

"And?"

"Everything looks fine. Nothing to worry about." His eyes didn't match his words. Was he just sad for me, or did he not want to add to the waterfall of stress I was drowning under?

"You can tell me if something's wrong. If you're sick or something, I don't want you holding back on my account. Frankly, I'd rather know now. I'm already losing Calvin. If I'm going to lose you too, I'd like to prepare for that."

"Wow, that's morbid." He took my hand in his. "There's nothing else to tell."

"Promise?"

"Promise."

The world around me is burning, yet at this moment, I feel a semblance of peace. My eyes lock with John's. Rays of hope overtake the sadness in our eyes. We lean in and I can feel his breath on me.

"Are you both planning on staying out there all evening?" Charlotte shouts behind us.

My cheeks flush and I push myself off the ground. "We're coming." I hold out my hand for John.

He smiles as he rises to his feet and leads me into the house.

"Can you give Olivia and I a moment?" Charlotte asks, leaning up against the door frame.

Once John was out of earshot, she continued. "I'm sorry. Did I interrupt something?" Her smile goes from ear to ear.

"Yes, you did. So nothing happened. Thank you for that."

"Shit. Sorry. But it will happen, right?"

"I'm in a horrible place. When I'm in a horrible place, I get close to the wrong people. Do you remember what I let happen with William?"

"That was different."

"Was it? Emotionally fragile and lost, I try to avoid my truth by turning to the arms of a man made of secrets. John's hiding something, I know it. From my point of view, not that different."

"Can you ever trust anyone?" She asks.

"No."

"Fine, but can I ask one thing?"

"What?"

"When was the last time you had sex?"

"Charlotte!"

"All I'm saying is, there aren't a lot of eligible bachelors your age around here. John's a nice guy - or so he seems. And fragile or not, you need a night of passionate sex. Perhaps, a distraction is what the Reverend ordered."

"I'm going now."

"I'm not wrong."

"You're not right either."

Even more flustered after talking with Charlotte, my cheeks are burning. I toss the blanket aside and avoid John.

Charlotte takes a swig of wine and takes control of the situation. "With our escapees back, let's talk about what I could find. First, I've confirmed the alteration of the photos. My experts compared pixels per unit, or whatever it is, and the knife and the rest of the picture don't match. Although the image of the knife is indistinguishable as being a layered item in the picture, it uses fewer pixels than the rest of the elements in the photo. Ray, I'll get you the name of the specialist so they can walk you through everything and you'll have a list of questions to ask your experts."

"Great." Ray's foot bounces under the table. The reverberations travel up my chair.

"Second, and just as important, is the finger print we found on the tip of the knife-"

"What print?" Ray asks.

"Didn't I tell you? There was a partial print that didn't match Calvin or Olivia on the knife. It looks like the police never ran it."

"Did you get a match?" John asks.

"No. But there is enough there that if we find the owner, we should be able to match it."

"So it's not Doctor Harrison's?" I ask.

"Her prints weren't in any database. Which is odd, as all medical practitioners have to have them on file for insurance. Which brings me to an interesting piece of information. The prints on file for one Matilda Harrison are Helen Hammond's."

All these years later, and the name still sends chills down my spine. "For the love of God, tell me that Matilda is not Helen's twin, otherwise I will strangle you for not telling me sooner."

"Not twins. They're five years apart. And different mothers, remember?"

"The Hammonds altered information all the time. It is plausible you have a mole in your organization covering tracks and laying other ones."

Charlotte purses her lips and inhales a long breath through her nose.

"Sorry, I didn't mean that."

"Yes, you did. And that's okay. I triple checked the information to verify the same thing. No moles. That's not important right now. What is important is, if she is alive, finding her and proving the print on the knife is hers."

"And how do you propose we do that?" I ask.

Charlotte turns to Ray. "Any chance your therapist can plug into those memories? Get some of the information about their meetings?"

"I can try, but Calvin seems pretty focused on the murder."

I slam my palm on the table. "Tell him his life depends on it, and force him to listen."

Ray slumps in his chair. "Again, I'll try. However, let's say we do find this M, who could be Matilda. What will a partial print prove? If I'm a jury member, it will not convince me that a kid who can remember murdering Shaylynn didn't do it, because of a partial print. I believe our best bet is a plea deal."

"STOP IT! STOP IT! STOP IT! Stop saying Calvin murdered Shaylynn. I don't care if that's what he thinks happened. I don't care if that is what the evidence says. Even if I'm starting to believe all of this, I don't want to hear it! He will not plead guilty. Now, you said you won't have to submit the therapy sessions. So there goes that admission. If you put him on the stand, I'll kill you, so no risk there. Now all you need to do is bring doubt to the Crown's evidence, and find him not guilty. What the fuck are we paying you for? A plea deal, my ass."

Ray straightens. Sweat pours down his temples and his pupils widen.

"What Olivia is trying to say-"

"John shut up. I said what I meant. You should know me better than to assume otherwise. Unless our friend here has something to hide, he should follow up on Charlotte's information and bring my son home."

"I was trying to be realistic and-" The cell phone in front of Ray rings. "I need to take this. Why don't I head out and follow up with you all once I've gone over the new information?"

"Thanks, Ray." Charlotte shouts after him.

I poke John in the ribs. "Follow him."

"What? Why?" John asks.

"He's hiding something," I say.

"You always think-"

"Go or he will be gone before you can figure out who he's talking to." I nudge him off his chair.

Charlotte and I hide behind the curtains of the living room window while John scrambles out the door. John startles Ray and causes him to drop his phone. John picks it up and hands it back. We can't hear what they say, but it sounds heated.

Ray punches John and smashes his head on the roof of the car. Charlotte and I bolt out the front door, but Ray has driven away before we get outside.

"What happened?" we ask in unison.

Blood drips down John's face. "The caller ID said M."

CHAPTER TWENTY-EIGHT

OLIVIA

"The phone said 'M', you saw the whole screen?" The person we are counting on to get my son out of jail is working for the other side. My scalp screams as I pull my hair. This isn't happening.

"Yes. It had (Mom) after it, but he still labeled it as M. That can't be a coincidence. And who puts 'mom' in brackets? Like, a person doesn't know who their mom is on their phone?"

I turn to Charlotte. "He came on your recommendation. I thought you vetted him? Tell me he is not somehow involved in this?"

"I vetted him. There has to be a mistake. What exactly did he say when you asked him about it?"

"He said his mother's name was Mary, and it was none of my business."

"Why did he punch you?" I ask.

"And smash your face against the car?" Charlotte follows up.

"I told him that if they found Calvin guilty, he would have more than you two to deal with."

My stomach flutters, knowing John's standing up for my son. "And he attacked you for that?" I ask.

"Perhaps he has an unpleasant history with clergy. He told me to fuck off, became aggressive, and drove away."

"Charlotte, I don't like this. Vetted, or no, we should get another lawyer?"

"This close to the trial? Let me do some more digging. We missed Helen's fingerprints on file for Doctor Harrison. I hate to say it, but it's possible we missed something else. Let's keep Ray representing Calvin for now, so we can monitor him. If he is against us, and shows up, I'd rather have him close by, hoping to pick up on his next move. Much better to plan for the known rather than the unknown. Keep your enemies close. I'll find a co-counsel to join the team. This way, we aren't relying on one lawyer."

"Good idea. Any chance we can move this conversation inside so I can get this blood off of me?" John asks.

"I'll get back on the phone. Olivia, why don't you help John." Charlotte doesn't even try to hide the wink.

John sits on the toilet while I try to be gentle, cleaning the blood from his nose and the cut on his forehead. He only winces once, but he keeps clenching and unclenching his hands.

"Nothing's broken, and that cut isn't too deep, so I don't think you need stitches." I say.

"Thank you doctor, I appreciate your medical attention. Now if you could examine this bunion on my foot." John sticks his foot straight out.

"Hilarious. You should have a shower." I toss first aid wrappers into the garbage and give John room to get off the toilet.

"Do I smell?" He pretends to sniff each armpit. "Lemony fresh."

"Your shirt wasn't victim-less in the blood battle, so you likely have some under it. Plus, lying around in the grass earlier," my cheeks get warm. "Anyway, I thought you'd want to get cleaned up. I can grab you a fresh shirt." I leave before John can respond.

John is staying in the spare bedroom at the other end of the hallway.

I pull out a shirt from the dresser drawer. I smile. The Clash. Are all the T-shirts John owns of 80's rock bands? Shower curtain rings scrape the shower rod, water pelts the tub, and the shower curtain slides closed, echoing down the hallway.

Should I poke my head into the bathroom and toss the shirt on the counter? What if I see something I don't want to? Or something I do? Stop it Olivia. You're not in the right head space to be thinking about having sex with your Reverend. Oh Lord, thinking that is gross. Friend. It's not the right time to be thinking about having sex with your friend.

Even if it would be nice to forget everything for a little while, it's been so long I'm not sure I remember what to do. Okay, erasing all sexual thoughts from my mind and putting his shirt on the bed. I'll go downstairs and catch up with Charlotte. A woman that beautiful has to have a sex life I can live vicariously through.

The moment I step into the hallway, so does John, in nothing but a towel. He's no model, but I cannot stop staring at the definition of his stomach muscles. Where did those come from? I swear I've seen him on the beach and not once were these revealed to me. If they had... For Christ's sake, Olivia, stop it. Walk away. Now!

"Hi," John says.

I drag my eyes to his. "Hi."

"So that T-shirt?" he asks.

"On the bed. You started the water, so I didn't want to interrupt you," I say.

"I wouldn't have minded," he replies.

"Haha." I drop the ends of the hair I'm twirling. "Progressing straight from a failed kiss to me walking in on you in a shower. Is that how you treat a lady?"

"Only if she wants me to," he says.

"Are you drunk?" The sweat from my palms won't come off on my pants.

"I might be. The alcohol has been flowing. Does it matter if I might be tipsy?" he responds.

"I'm curious. You're being very forward and you never talk to me like this."

He steps before me. Water drips down his body.

"Perhaps it took me years to realize life is too short to not go after what I want." John's warm hand brushes my hair away from my face and pulls my chin up. His supple lips taste like the wine he'd been drinking. As we kiss, he guides

121

me back into his room and closes the door, not once removing his lips from mine. His towel falls to the floor, followed feverishly by my clothes. I'd almost forgotten what the caress of a man's hands over my body feels like. Every nerve is on fire. Begging for more. He stops, his body on top of mine, and stares. "You're beautiful."

"You already have me naked. No need to flatter me," I say.

He laughs, kisses me, and takes his lips on a trip down my chest and between my legs. I grip the sheets as wave after wave of pleasure comes over me. His lips. His tongue. Perfection. My hips thrust high, and my eyes roll back into my head. Euphoria! John rises and entwines his body with mine. Any part of us that can touch the other does. Our bodies meld into one. The hairs on my arms float to the sky as his fingers brush my skin. I've never felt like this before and I don't want it to stop. His eyes peer into my soul, and I sense that I'm safe.

I find Charlotte in the kitchen, pouring over more files and focusing on a particular piece of paper. She rubs her eyes when she notices me.

"You're alive," she says.

"Shut up." I run the tap until the water is ice cold, and fill two glasses.

"All that thumping. I thought you'd be out cold. Or raring for seconds," Charlotte says.

"You could hear all that? Oh god." My cheeks become warm. I place one of the cold glasses against my cheek to cool my embarrassment.

"This is an old house with thin walls. I heard everything," Charlotte says.

"Lovely. Well, then you should already know that I got seconds," I say.

"Haha. That good, huh?" Charlotte asks.

"Um, yeah. Although, I'm no expert but, yeah."

"You look happy." She smiles.

"As happy as I can be, considering. What are you reading?" I ask.

"Nothing." She scrambles to hide the paperwork.

"It's obviously something, if you're trying to hide it." I move beside her.

"It can wait until morning. It's not that important." Charlotte tucks the folder under the tall stack on the table.

"Well, if it isn't that important, why not share it with me? My life is 99% shit. I doubt you can take away the 1% that isn't."

"I wouldn't be so sure about that."

The cups of water find a new home on the table. I pull the file from the bottom of the stack. "What's this?"

"It's a file on John," Charlotte replies.

Page after page of John's life is in my hands. I turn through the pages until my fingers freeze, holding the corner of a page near the back of the file. "Why do you have his medical records?"

"A thorough check means we review everything," She responds.

"Right. And what is a GI tumor? It can't be good." My shallow breathing turns rapid.

"It means he has cancer," she advises.

"He told me his doctor said he was fine." Weakness in my legs forces me to sit down across from Charlotte.

"He probably doesn't want to worry you with everything else you have going on," Charlotte says.

"First, he hides his mother from me and now he has cancer. What else hasn't he told me?" I ask myself more than Charlotte.

"Let's not overreact-"

"You want to see me overreact? Wait until he gets down here." The subsided anger resurfaces.

"Maybe people keep secrets from you because, whether the information is good or bad, you react poorly. Or, the fact people make one mistake and you lose all trust in them. You've been through some shit, but that doesn't mean the entire world is out to get you. Who is the one person, next to me, who has stood by you after finding out about everything that happened to you? Who is the one person who will stop mid-conversation to say hi when you arrive at a gathering? And who is the one person who puts up with your bullshit? If that isn't love, what is?"

Charlotte's right. John's always been here for me, even through all my difficulties. Yet, the voice inside me is telling me there's more I don't know. My gut is always right. I need to find out what I am missing

Chapter Twenty-Nine

Calvin

It's been two weeks and I haven't had another therapy session. This is so frustrating! How does anyone expect me to remember what happened, if the person who can help me do that doesn't visit? Mr. Bower keeps saying I'm not her only client and it might be best to wait until the trial is over before I have any more sessions. What's he afraid I'll figure out?

I've been trying to go back through the events myself, but nothing is working. I can't figure out who the figure in black is, who the blurry person is, or where the knife comes from. Everything I need to get me out of this shit hole!

Knuckles rattle against my open cell door, "Lyons, you have a visitor." Marc says. His guard's uniform is fresh and ironed.

"Who is it?" I ask.

"Your mom," he answers.

"I don't want to see her," I grumble.

"Kid, see your mom. Don't roll your eyes at me. Moms can be all we get sometimes. Given you are in here for murder, I doubt you will have many other visitors. Besides, you don't want to alienate the one person who believes in you, do you? Let's go." Marc says.

Believe in me, my ass. When she looks at me, all she sees is my father. She doesn't think I can tell, but the twitches of her lip, and the quick glances away, tell me otherwise. It's as if she's trying to reset the view she sees. And why does everyone think all moms are wonderful, anyway? There are a lot of shitty moms in the world, and mine isn't so great.

The common area is full. As usual. I ignore everyone. As usual. A few whispers trail behind me, but everyone has left me alone since the fight in the cafeteria.

"Stop dragging your feet. Walk like a regular person," Marc says.

"Regular people drag their feet." I exaggerate the action.

"Please, pick up your feet while you walk, and save all of our ears," he says.

Annoyance is achieved, but I don't get any satisfaction from it. I stop dragging my feet, and for the rest of the walk, Marc's quiet. That is, until we got to the visitor's center's door.

"Is that your mom?" Marc asks.

"Well, she's the only one in there, so yeah, that's my mom," I say.

"She's cute," he states.

"Gross."

"I'm just saying, you could have a worse-looking mom."

"I could also have a better looking guard," I say.

"I like you, kid." Marc says with a wink. "Be nice."

"Yeah, okay."

The whirring of the pop and snack machines replaces the door buzzings and bustle of the inner prison, and the flickering of a florescent light in the far corner draws my eye. I can only dawdle so long before I get to Mom's table. She stands and opens her arms. I keep my hands in my pockets, sit at the table, and stare at the wall past her.

"Thank you for seeing me. I wasn't sure if-"

"Whatever. I needed to get out of my cell," I say.

"The bruises are healing nicely," she says.

"Yeah." The blacks and blues have faded into greens and yellows.

"Look, there are some things you need to know. About your case," she advises.

"Mmm." I'd rather be anywhere but here.

"We found some things that could help you." A pinch of excitement lives in Mom's voice.

"Really?" My focus shifts from the wall to her.

Mom continues. "The photos of you with the knife, they're not real."

Punched in the gut, I grip the table to keep myself upright. "What do you mean, they're not real?"

"Photos were taken without you holding the knife, and it was added later." She answers.

"Why? Who?" I ask.

Mom moves from the seat opposite me to the one beside. "To retaliate against me."

"You?"

"There are a few things I haven't told you," Mom says.

"A few?" The mountain of secrets Mom kept from me amounted to more than a few.

"Yes. Things you don't tell a child. But, I'll tell you now. You can get mad at me all you want; but I need you to promise me something," she says.

"Of course you do," I say.

"Honey, please. This 'M' person-"

"Mr. Bower told you!"

"No, he didn't. Someone I presume to be M, sent me a letter. I need you to promise me you won't see her again. She's very dangerous and is using you against me."

"Wow, you think you know everything; but you don't. Whoever you think M is, it's not them. M isn't a woman."

Mom rubs her face and her voice becomes deflated. "So, M is a man?"

"Yes."

"You're sure?" Mom pulls out a photo of a woman in her fifties who stands in front of a large manor house. "You've never seen this woman? She'd be older now."

"I don't know who that is," I say.

Mom wrings the photo between her hands until it tears in two. My heart yearns to comfort her, but the anger inside me wins out. I keep my hands to myself.

"It could be someone working with her. If Doctor Harrison, the woman from the photo, is involved, you need to understand the monster she is. What I'm about to tell you may sound unbelievable, but please listen carefully. This is the woman, whom I know to be Doctor Matilda Harrison, who performed your c-section. After which, she left me cut open to die. She found out I'd been a cop and wanted revenge for all the damage I'd done to her sister's business and reputation. Her sister was your father's Aunt.. Helen ran the Hammond operation here in Europe and I helped Charlotte get evidence to shut it all down. Or at least most of it. Hence the revenge."

Is Mom for real with this story? "If this is all true, why were you with the Hammonds in the first place? Did you work for them or something?" I ask.

"It's complicated and we don't have enough time for me to tell you the entire story," she responds.

"Of course not," I say.

"I promise, when this is over, I will tell you everything, so far as you want to hear it. For now, the articles you had in your room about William were accurate. What they didn't say was that I killed your father after the trial. I also killed William's brother, Adam, in Los Angeles, before William forced me to come to England," Mom says.

"So, M hadn't lied about you murdering my father. Great, both my parents are murderers, I'm fucking doomed," I say.

"No, you're not. William ordered my sister's death, and Adam carried it out. I killed them for her, as well as to guarantee my freedom. You know what William's, well, all the Hammond's business was about, right?" she asks.

"Yeah."

"I was one of their victims. I was kidnapped, and forced to service men and women while they profited. And it wasn't just me. There were others in Los Angeles with me. We escaped and burned William's house to the ground. We thought he was inside and that we were free." Tears wash Mom's face. "You're the only reason I'm alive, and I thank God every day for that. We might not get along, but you're my entire world."

"The articles said you married William. Why? That makes no sense," I say.

"It embarrassed William that he failed in Los Angeles and, to protect you, he couldn't tell anyone who I was. They would have killed us all. So we pretended we were in a relationship. Then, out of nowhere, he proposes at a large party, in front of hundreds of guests, and I'm forced to say yes. Any other answer and-"

"You'd be dead."

"Exactly. Do what they want or die is how I lived for five months in England. To survive, I did what I had to do. I'd say I'm not proud of it, but I am. When many people around the world don't, I got out. I helped bring down one of the most comprehensive human trafficking rings in the world, and saved thousands of people from falling victim to the Hammonds. Do you see now, why whoever this person is that gave you those articles, might be manipulating you against me?"

"They're not manipulating me!" I exclaim.

"Do you honestly believe you could have killed Shaylynn? You loved her," Mom says.

"I remember!" I yell.

"Do you? I've heard about the sessions, and it's hard to separate fact from reality. Maybe what you remember isn't real at all." She holds my hand. This time I didn't pull away.

"How?" I ask.

"I'm not an expert, but it sounds like your memories are all jumbled together. You're also afraid you really did it, so maybe your brain is tricking you into thinking you did it. You've seen the evidence and your mind is placing it in your memories as you try to make sense of everything," she says.

"But my fingerprints are on the knife," I say.

"Yes, but they sit on top of the blood. This might happen for one or two prints, but not all of them. If you were holding the knife while you stabbed Shaylynn, your prints would be under some of the blood," Mom explains.

This is all too much. The room spins. I rest my head on my hands in front of me. Mom rubs my back. It feels nice. Like when we used to watch movies together.

She continues, "it'll be okay. We'll figure all this out."

129

Inhaling all the air I can, I sit up. There was one question I needed answered. "Did you ever think I did it?"

Mom's jaw slacks. "Honey, no. I. . ." Her head hangs low. "Yes. I did."

My fists collide with the metal table. "My mother thinks I'm a murderer!" I can't stay in this room with her anymore. I stand and Mom clings to the sleeve of my sweater.

"Please, listen. I only thought that because I feared William, not you. I've always feared you would turn out like him. That's why I kept everything from you for so long. I don't know why, but I thought if you knew the truth, it would trigger something in you, and then, well, we would be where we are now," she explains.

"Trigger something? That sounds ridiculous," I say.

"It's irrational, I know. After all the death, destruction, and torture I saw, I couldn't stop myself from thinking it could happen," Mom says quietly.

Tears stream down Mom's cheeks and puddle on her shirt. More proof this is all her fault, but it was mine too. I free myself from her grasp and back away from the table. I need to get out of jail and the only way is with Mom's help, whether she sees me as a murderer or not.

"Do you still think I did it?" I ask.

"Heavens no. It was only a fleeting thought. I'm doing everything I can to prove you're innocent," she says.

Not telling her about M is getting me nowhere. If I tell her, hopefully, she can find him and then bring me home. "I don't know where he, M, is. He's older. Broad shoulders. Like a rugby player. Brown hair. He's very stern when he talks. We always met somewhere around Coltam," I advise.

"So that means he probably lives close by. If he's been watching us for years, he wouldn't travel far to do it," Mom says.

I recount what I can of my meetings with M. "I'll tell Mr. Bower to tell you everything. I may have forgotten some stuff."

"About Mr. Bower. I'm not sure we can trust him," she says.

Is there anyone on this fucking earth I can trust?

Mom continues, "Charlotte is looking into him again, so keep acting normal, but be careful."

"Won't he get me convicted if he's against us?" I ask.

"I won't let that happen. I have a plan," she answers.

Chapter Thirty

Stranger

Feet pound behind me and stop. My running companion is bent over his knees, coughing and out of breath. His dark hair is in disarray. "You're late. I've run this stretch three times waiting for you."

Words creep out between breaths. "Sorry. I needed to wrap up a few things before I could get over here." He runs his fingers through his hair and tames the mess.

"Did you take care of the therapist?" I ask.

"Yes. No one will find her."

"Good. Now, what are you doing about Charlotte interfering with the case?"

"There is a simple solution, but you won't let me handle it that way, so I'm stuck in a corner."

First, he didn't want to kill the therapist, now he wants to kill everyone. "We've been over this. If Charlotte dies or goes missing, you cannot stop people from asking questions. Find a new way to silence her."

"Short of tying her up and gagging her, I'm not sure there is anything we can do. She'll never let doctored evidence be used in court. At minimum, she'll talk to the Crown prosecutor and advise them of her suspicions. They won't bring up anything that would call their integrity into question. Even if they can't prove the photos are fake. They'll take their time to review everything rather than make a fool of themselves."

"There's a conflict of interest angle you could point to. The best friend of the mother of the defendant, investigating the crime, is not exactly ethical. We've worked together on this for years. How am I the only one coming up with actionable solutions? You're useless."

"I'm sorry Father. I guess I've been preoccupied."

"Well, focus, otherwise everything we worked for will fall apart. Does Olivia know about Shaylynn's diary entries?"

"I don't think so," Buck says.

"Good, maybe when that comes out, it will keep her and Charlotte looking in another direction for a while."

"You know Olivia almost better than she does. Do you think she's going to stop looking for us with the revelation of the diaries?"

"The entries, and if Calvin testifies-"

"He won't. Olivia and Charlotte will make sure of that."

"There has to be a way you can convince him it would be better for him to share his story. Free his conscience. Set his soul free."

"Calvin gets on that stand, and Olivia's wrath will come for everyone."

"Well, you need to make sure she doesn't find me. Or figure out who you are."

"I'm trying! I hate to admit it, but your letter was an excellent distraction, but they'll realize Doctor Harrison is dead soon enough. Once they do, they'll turn to the next person on their list."

"I guess it's a good thing no one can trace any information to find out that I exist. Or that you're a Hammond."

"Something else you should be aware of, our friend is getting a little jittery, but I'll get her back in line."

"It sounds like she's a loose end we're going to need to wrap up after all of this."

"She's a good kid, so let's just keep the option of her surviving open. She's just nervous because she doesn't know where she's getting the tips from and who she's helping."

Buck's always been compassionate, a trait that got a lot of Hammonds in trouble. I don't feel like lecturing him today, so I leave it alone. There is too much to do before the trial. I need to ensure everything's set up, so I can watch Olivia's life shatter into pieces on the courtroom floor.

CHAPTER THIRTY-ONE

OLIVIA

L ife has been a whirlwind since Calvin's arrest, two months ago. I've had no time to breathe, barely slept and have eaten so little I've lost ten pounds. I torture myself every day for ever thinking Calvin killed Shaylynn. It'll be hard to forgive myself for turning against my son.

For eighteen years, all I saw was William before me. Not my son. I never gave him a chance to show me he was different. That he was his own person.

John rolls onto his side and faces me. His eyes remain closed and his breath is heavy. I don't know how he can sleep. Then again, dealing with me can be exhausting. If only I could sleep through this, and wake up to find everything fixed.

I rub my finger along the faint scar behind my ear. I don't have to see it to visualize the H shape it takes. Now and then, when I wear my hair up, people ask me about it. I give the same answer I gave Calvin, a hair straighter hit the same spot. I'm not sure if anyone believes me, but they don't prod any further.

John knows the truth. John knows my every truth.

I turn onto my side and stare at him. Each wrinkle under his eyes is a line of a story lived. The strands of grey in his hair peek out from their hiding place under the mountains of black. He looks ten years younger than his fifty-two years. My fingertips kiss his thick locks.

The way he sleeps, with his mouth open a bit, makes me want to wake him with a kiss. However, he's so peaceful, I don't want to disturb him. Grief wells up inside of me. I try to control my breathing and calm myself so my shaking doesn't wake him.

Alienated by the town, John has no one to turn to. No one to help him fight his illness. If only he would tell me. My life is shit right now, but I can still help.

Every other year, someone in town is sick, and chooses to handle it on their own. Miracles have happened, but most of the people lie in the cemetery outside John's church. When I visit John at church, I want it to be to hear him speak, not to place flowers in front of a stone.

I'm trying hard to respect his choice not to tell me he has cancer. Yet, I want to shake him violently and ask why. How long can I watch from a distance while someone who has taken care of me for years goes through treatment, or heaven forbid dies, alone?

I roll onto my back. The pink and orange sunrise paints my crisp white ceiling.

I should tell him I'm aware. I don't want him to worry about causing me stress; however, the burden of trying to not let on that I know is heavy. Why does love have to be so fucking hard?

Whoa, love?

I haven't loved a man since, well, ever. There was my old police partner, Joe, but I was never 'in-love' with him. Man, I wish I could call him. He'd know what to do. Or at least caution me about what not to do. And then I would do exactly that. Wherever he is, I hope the Witness Protection Program has treated him, and his family, well.

John snorts and hits my chest with his arm as he flops it over me. He's sprawled out like a starfish. I want to lie like this forever. Maybe it is love? When did that happen? Nothing's changed. Well, sex, but that doesn't equal love. A picture of him waiting for me in a suit at the end of the church aisle dances above me in the sunlight. Fuck, I'm in trouble if I'm pondering marriage. I can't marry a dying man. No. He might not be dying. The internet said this cancer is treatable. I'll have to believe it, as my doctor will no longer see me, so I can't ask her. John can't die. He won't die. I'll not allow it. I need him.

I hug his arm. John moans, but his eyes remain closed. If I stay in bed any longer, tears will wash John's arm. I crawl out from under him unnoticed. The stairs creak. I stop. John's still asleep.

I lean against the living room window, steam from my tea crawls up the window. Woodhaven looks peaceful from up here. Someone is running up the hill to my house. When they reach the edge of my driveway, my heart sinks to the bottom of my stomach, and I know the peace I felt moments ago is gone.

Chapter Thirty-Two

Olivia

I'm surprised it took Ernest Taylor this long to come see me. Our brief encounter on the street corner wasn't half of the verbal beating I thought he would deliver. Calvin's trial starting tomorrow must have given him the backbone he needed to confront the mother of the boy accused of killing his daughter.

Gravel spits as he runs up my driveway. Ernest bites his bottom lip, fists form at his sides, and his eyes sear through my windowpane. I open my door before he can break it down. "Why don't we talk outside? People are sleeping," I say.

"I don't care," Ernest says.

I push past him and close the door behind me. He storms over to me and slaps me. My cheek and my hand burn. One from Ernest and one from the spilled scalding tea.

"You will not get away with this," he shouts.

"Get away with what?" I ask.

"You think because you have friends in high places, they will just make this all disappear? Tamper with evidence. Where is Charlotte anyway? I want to talk to her too," Ernest says.

"She's in London. What are you talking about, tampering with evidence?" I ask.

"I know you'd go to any length to free your son. A murderer!" He yells.

"Calvin didn't-"

"Yes, he did! Calvin killed my Shaylynn and I won't let him get away with it. Not after what he did to my little girl!" Ernest lunges at me.

My back hits the ground hard, with two-hundred-plus pounds on top of me. My mug flies over my head and shatters on the grass behind. Ernest sits on top of me. I try to push him off, but I'm not strong enough. I punch as hard as I can, with no reaction from him. His anger is a shield to my fists. He pins my hips and legs with his body mass. Finger by finger, he wraps both hands around my neck. Teeth gritted, he squeezes. The whites of his eyes are bloodshot with anger. I struggle to free myself. There's no air. The blue sky above is being eaten away by grey. It closes in at the center of my vision. Ernest's hands are still around my neck as I'm pulled upwards. He lets go. I topple to the side, gasping for air.

John yells, "Leave her be!"

Ernest elbows John's side and pushes himself to his feet. "You shouldn't be helping evil souls like her, Reverend. Let me handle her."

"You know I can't do that." John, in only his underwear, brushes the grass off his legs.

"You've made your choice." Ernest charges at him.

Each man gets in punches as they roll towards the hedge and the edge of the property. The tips of the grass are painted with a trail of blood that follows the men.

My phone is in the house. I pray Ernest won't kill John before I can get to it. I've experienced the same rage. It's what led me to kill Adam and William. Once it takes over, it's hard to calm it.

When I get back outside, the police are on their way, but John lies flat on the ground and isn't moving.

Ernest looks at me over his shoulder. "You're next!" He comes at me like a bull. I dodge and jump off the front stoop. Ernest trips. Gnomes collide with his head as I run towards the backyard. Sirens wail in the distance. Ernest's not deterred. He grabs my wrist and spins me towards him. He pushes me up against the side of the house. The layered siding digs into my back. His body is pressed against mine, his hands grip both sides of my head, and he yanks it forward. SMASH! Pain shoots through the back of my head and through my eyes. He pulls my head forward again. "You and your son took my girl's life, and I will take both of yours."

"Ernest, step back from Olivia." DI Whitaker's enormous frame stands a few feet from Ernest.

Without taking his eyes off me, Ernest replies. "Daniel, let me finish this."

Two officers appear over Ernest's shoulders and try to pull him back. He won't let go of my head. But his body has parted from mine. WHACK! My knee meets Ernest's crotch. He lets go and hits the ground. That felt good.

I ignore the officers and run to John. He's upright and massaging his head. Officer Cole is with him. "Are you all right?"

"Fine, he just knocked me out. Are you okay? Is that blood?" John asks.

The back of my head is sticky to the touch. Dark red spots appear on my fingers. "I'll be fine."

"If that's fine, what's hurt?" John asks.

"Stop worrying about me. It's Calvin we need to think about." I say.

"Calvin, why?"

Before I can answer, DI Whitaker comes over. "I'm sure you can see where he was coming from in all of this." Officers place Ernest in the back of a police vehicle. He glares at me as they back out of the drive. "We'll settle him down and make sure he doesn't come back here."

Was he serious? "How do you recommend that you do that? Are you going to have a car parked out front of my house? Follow me around town? You heard him threaten me, and you aren't taking it seriously," I say.

"I'll talk to him," DI Whitaker said.

"Ah yes, a conversation will surely quench his anger. Good luck with that." I reply.

DI Whitaker goes to speak, but decides against it. Instead, he leaves.

"Do either of you want me to take you to the hospital?" Officer Cole asks.

"We'll be fine, thank you," I say.

John waits for them to drive off before asking the obvious question. "What's going on with Calvin?"

"Ernest wants to kill him."

CHAPTER THIRTY-THREE

CALVIN

Marc keeps coming to see me when he's working. His muscular build is unmistakable in my peripheral vision. Sometimes he just passes by, other times, he sneaks me snacks or graphic novels. I hope he doesn't think I'll put in a good word for him with Mom. There's no way I'm letting him anywhere near her. He's too... I don't know. Weird? Whatever, not going to happen.

Today, he brought me a suit and dress shoes. "You'll get the tie at the courthouse."

"But I get the laces in my shoes?"

"Those cheap things will break if you tug them too hard. There's no concern about you killing yourself with those."

"Right."

"Well, get dressed."

"Plan on watching me the whole time?"

"You're doing nothing to help the smart-mouthed teenager stereotype. Hurry." He turns and talks to a nearby guard.

The polyester shirt chaffs against my skin. Even without the tie, the clothes suffocate me.

The bus to the courthouse has three riders. Two other inmates are staggered three seats apart, playing with the collars of unfamiliar clothing. I sit up front and ignore them. I focus on the pedestrians sweeping past as we drive through town.

The holding room at the courthouse reminds me of a miniature classroom. It even has a dry-erase whiteboard at the front. One guard stands inside the room, another stands outside. Court officers usher the others out of the room within twenty minutes of our arrival.

I wait. And wait. An hour later, and with my regrown cuticles clawed out, it's my turn. The other two haven't returned.

The door to the courtroom opens. I'm inundated by sensations I've never felt before. The courtroom lights are brighter than the holding room lights, and I can't stop myself from looking at the ground. I don't want to appear guilty; however, the light burns my eyes. Whispers buzz around me like bees. Some of the crowd sting me with their murmurs of "Murderer!"

My stomach fills with knots of dread fighting each other. Which fear will win out?

Fear 1: The evidence presented will convince a jury, and myself, that without a doubt, I killed Shaylynn.

Fear 2: That I'll soon lose the life I had, despite wishing I could escape it, and trade it in for lifetime accommodation in jail.

Fear 3: That I'll lose myself and turn into the shell of a person I've had to become to get through the past two months.

Until I crossed into the bland, cream and pale wood-coloured courtroom, I was in denial about what a trial meant. Whatever happens in this room will change my life forever, and I have little control over the results. The knots in my stomach tighten.

I raise my head and before I can locate my mom, my eyes fall on Shaylynn's parents. Mr. Taylor scowls and runs his fingers through his hair. The veins of his neck are visible across the room. Mrs. Taylor buries her face in her husband's chest. She wipes her eyes with a tissue and sobs. She doesn't look at me.

I find where Mom's sitting. I almost don't recognize her, dressed in a dark suit and make-up. She never dresses up and I don't recall her owning any makeup. Mom's sullen and reaches for John's hand beside her.

I'm put into a rectangular wooden box that stands as tall as my hips with glass walls twice my height. Scratches and prints tint the glass. Although there is no lid, I'm a zoo animal in a cage in my cell, but here, I'm a freak feature at a circus. Instead of being the bearded lady or world's tallest man, I'm the boy about to be set aflame to see if he'll live. They should charge twenty-five pence to watch.

Although I'm encased in wood and glass, the surrounding sounds filter through the gap between the top of the wood and bottom of the glass. I will hear whatever those say for or against me.

The court clerks are expressionless and their black robes sway as they move with experienced precision. The Judge's elevated seat waits to be filled with the holder of my future.

A man dressed in a black robe, white curled wig and a white tailed tie approaches me. His features are softened by the worn glass. "I'm Randall Tokarz. One of your lawyers."

"Where's Mr. Bower?" I ask.

"He'll be here. Your mom and aunt have added me on as co-counsel. Has Ray told you how all this is going to work?"

I nod.

"Good. Things may seem scary right now, and they are. However, having seen everything Charlotte and your mother have put together, we have a fighting chance. Don't lose faith, but say your prayers, as I won't lie to you kid, the justice system isn't always just."

At least he was honest.

"Sorry I'm late." Mr. Bower rushes past us in a similar outfit to Mr. Tokarz. Surrounded by robes and wigs, I've been transported back to the time of colonialism. Mr. Bower organizes his paperwork beside Mr. Tokarz, and then joins the conversation.

"Randall." Mr. Bower's voice is flat. "Calvin, you don't have to do much today. Just look sad and scared. No matter what the Crown prosecutor says, don't show any anger. The judge and jury will watch for how you react."

"Got it."

Mr. Bower walks over to Mom. "Where's Charlotte?"

"With the Crown Prosecutor?"

Mr. Bower wipes his brow. "Then I guess I'm not late." He turns back to me. "Can I get you anything? There should be water in the box."

"I'm fine."

Charlotte and the Crown Prosecutor walk through the large oak double doors at the back of the courtroom. Aunt Charlotte's arms clutch her body as if they will hold her together. The prosecutor pulls at her black robe and rolls her shoulders.

"Ray, we need to talk," The prosecutor says through gritted teeth.

"Are we looking to talk about a better deal?"

Charlotte stands beside the defendant's box and I watch as she tries to set Mr. Bower's clothes on fire with her eyes.

"Let's go." The prosecutor nods and they march out of the courtroom.

Behind me, Charlotte consults with this new lawyer, Mr. Tokarz. He has the bailiff release me from my box, and, with my mom, the four of us head out of the courtroom the way I came into it.

The crowd gets anxious and murmurs grow louder. Reporters hurl questions, trying to uncover what's happening. Their guess is as good as mine.

They put us in a room with no chairs and a small table in the corner. I tap my fingers on my legs as I watch everyone else circle the room and each other. No one needs a chair.

"What's going on?" Mom asks.

"Well, Ray hasn't brought forward our concerns about the evidence," Charlotte says.

"I'll kill him!" Mom squeezes her hands into balls.

"That's not even the bad news. They're going to proceed with the trial."

"Using altered evidence? This is bullshit. How can they even do that? Please tell me whoever has set up Calvin hasn't paid off the prosecutor or judge. I can't go through that again."

"I don't think it's like that. She said she found similar discrepancies and could find plausible explanations. She thinks she has enough for a conviction."

The room spins. I slide down the wall and put my head between my knees. Mom kneels beside me. "Are you alright?" My eyes tell her what I can't say. Her warm lips kiss my forehead. She runs her hands down the side of my face and kisses me again.

Back on her feet, "Okay, so this means we need to find another way to win. Randall, go find Ray and the prosecutor. Make sure he is not pushing another deal. My son will not be in jail for any longer than the time this farce of a trial takes. I'd ask you to make the prosecutor see reason, but if Charlotte can't, all hope might be lost for you."

"Your show of faith is heart-warming. But yes, Charlotte can be a viper, and if her bite came out as a scratch, you're right, no sense trying again. At least not today. I'll let you know what I find out."

"What do we do about Ray?" Mom asks.

"He'll realize we're aware he hasn't shared our concerns. But he'll say he tried and right now we can't prove otherwise. As much as we don't like it, it doesn't prove he's against us." Charlotte said.

"You're right, I don't like this."

"Randall wrapped up his other case earlier than expected, so he will help. He was my first choice, but I just couldn't get him until now. He'll monitor Ray and report back."

"Keep our enemies close."

"Exactly. I'll text John what's happening. I'm sure he's going stir-crazy out there." Aunt Charlotte's fingers tap rapidly on her phone.

Mom and Aunt Charlotte's words fly around me like they have hit me on the head in a cartoon. Once their meaning settles in, I can see the writing on the wall. The trial is over before it begins.

"Honey? You okay down there? Everything's going to be fine-"

I can't contain my anger. My disappointment. "Fine! How is everything going to be fine? Nothing's changed."

"I know but-"

"But what? Don't tell me you have a plan? You said that already, and it didn't work. Face it, Mom, I'm going to jail for the rest of my life and there's nothing you or Aunt Charlotte can do about it. Maybe we should make a deal."

SLAP

My cheek stings, and then I register my mom's actions.

"Don't you ever talk about a deal. That's what Ray wants you to do and if he hears you talking like this, he...No, it will not happen."

"Why not? I killed Shaylynn, so shouldn't I go to jail?" The words jump off my tongue with no effort.

Both women freeze in place, their eyes wide and heads shaking. Mirror images of each other.

"We talked about this. What you remember may not be true." Mom says.

"It's true. I remember everything. I stood over her and stabbed her six times. That's how many stab wounds there are, right?"

Charlotte and Mom catch each other's eyes for a split second. No one had told me how many stab wounds Shaylynn had. Mr. Bower said the police wanted me to admit it on my own. More concrete evidence of guilt if I say something I shouldn't be aware of. Mom didn't tell me because she wanted to protect me.

But I knew.

My dreams are becoming so vivid that I feel the knife pierce the fabric of Shaylynn's T-shirt, cut through her skin and slide through her body.

I am a murderer.

Chapter Thirty-Four

Stranger

The air is stuffy and warm in the crowded courtroom. The breath of the person seated beside me smells of egg salad. Everyone is shoulder to shoulder, whether seated or standing. The only people given the respect of space, and only a few inches, are Mr. and Mrs. Taylor.

I slouch in a seat in the back row, on the aisle seat so as not to be seen by Calvin or his entourage. It's hard to do as there is little foot room and every time I move I rub up against my neighbour. My line of sight has a perfect view of Olivia. Her fingers tap her leg to the nervous music rattling inside her head.

My body is at equilibrium. No nervous ticks, knee jostling, or rapid heartbeat. All roads have led to where I sit today and will continue to lead to Olivia's destruction. One court date at a time.

The prosecutor looks like she wants to eat Ray Bower alive. She pulls him out of the room and I'm left wondering if there will be a trial at all. I suppose a plea deal will still get me the results I want. It would be disappointing to not watch Olivia crumble, piece by piece; however, my satisfaction will come from knowing I've ripped away her safety net, taken away the child she loves and, in the end, watched her die. Slowly and painfully.

My neighbour elbows me as he types on his phone. I jam his ribs hard and before he can protest, my eyes tell him he's better off saying nothing.

Olivia, Charlotte, Calvin, and whoever this new lawyer is, leave the room. John remains behind. Curious. Maybe he's relegated to a seat saver and is no longer as close to Olivia as I thought? Every minute they're gone, the temperature in the courtroom increases. The hot air that fills everyone heats the room, with theories of the reason for the delay. The crowd is becoming restless. Reporters and bystanders are itching for information.

Twenty minutes later, everyone returns and takes their positions in the courtroom. Mr. Taylor stands up when Calvin re-enters. His eyes throw daggers at Calvin, whose face is a sheet of white. For a moment, I feel sorry for the Taylors. But only for a moment. Someone had to be sacrificed to make my plan work.

Reporters try to ask questions of the prosecutor about the delay; however, a clerk's booming voice silences the room of sardine-stuffed occupants with "all rise".

Judge Parton's red robe guides the eyes of the courtroom as she sits and goes through the rules for both the participants and the crowd before calling the Crown Prosecutor forward to deliver their opening statement.

"Good morning My Lady, Ms. Klein for the Crown. We're here today to discuss the charge of murder set against Calvin Lyons. In the early morning hours of June 15, Shaylynn Taylor, a seventeen-year-old girl, walked into a forest with this man. It is there that he stabbed her six times. It was there that he left her, while he ran and tried to hide the evidence. A running shoe, covered in Shaylynn's blood, was found in a garbage bin less than a kilometer away. The murder weapon, a knife from Calvin Lyon's own kitchen, was found metres away. Calvin himself was found wandering the streets, covered in Shaylynn's blood."

"But why would this man take his friend's life? We intend to prove that Calvin was upset and angry that his *only* friend no longer wanted any sort of relationship with him. Calvin felt abandoned by his *only* friend, someone he was in love with, and he couldn't handle her leaving him. Calvin became obsessive and, despite being told by Shaylynn to leave her alone, he stalked her. We will show Shaylynn's diary entries, which recount the numerous times she was afraid of Calvin. How she even feared for her life."

"Shaylynn Taylor didn't run into Woodhaven forest on June 15 for fun. She went in there to get away from Calvin Lyons. Shaylynn feared for her life and the quickest way home was through that forest. Photos will show Calvin Lyons holding the murder weapon and Shaylynn running for safety. Trying to get home."

"The defense will claim Shaylynn and Calvin's friendship wasn't broken. In fact, they will show that Calvin and Shaylynn had consensual sex a day prior to her death. However, scared for their lives, teenagers will do things you or I would think irrational. A defense mechanism for protection. Shaylynn didn't have sex with Calvin because she wanted to. She had sex with him because she had to."

I can't help but smile. This prosecutor knows what she's doing. Every piece of the puzzle is being placed perfectly, and a picture of Olivia's demise is coming into focus. Not just for me, but for her as well. Olivia's finger taps against her leg, increasing speed with every sentence the prosecutor speaks. Olivia's head is on a swivel as she looks between her son, Charlotte, and John.

"The defense will also claim someone has tampered with some of the evidence. I assure you, we have completed a full review of everything and found nothing to support their claims. The Woodhaven Police Department and the Crown Prosecutors' office have meticulously handled the evidence."

"Once both sides have presented their findings, the evidence will show, beyond a doubt, that Calvin Lyons murdered Shaylynn Taylor."

The prosecutor takes her seat, and the whispers that erupted with the mention of Shaylynn's diary entries ripple through the room like waves crashing against each body from the front to the back. Frenzied fingers tap screens. The courtroom doors collide as eager reporters dash out of the room. Fresh evidence means a new headline.

It takes five minutes to get the crowd under control and even then, mumblings continue behind hand-covered mouths.

Ray Bower stands, and his words float past me, unheard. Olivia's hair flips behind her shoulder and a tug from my belly button pulls me to my feet. The chord between her and I shortens millimeter by millimeter. The crowd around me fades into a fog. There is only Olivia. My fingers tingle and desire to wrap themselves around her neck. I elongate and retract them in preparation. Only a few more feet.

Strong hands grip my arms. The dark-haired figure with recognizable eyes speaks to me without words.

Father, what are you doing

CHAPTER THIRTY-FIVE

OLIVIA

I've never heard Ray Bower sound as monotone as he does during his opening statement. Heads bob around me as though the air Ray's words travel on contains a comatose solution. I remain focused. Somewhere in all of this mess is a solution. Maybe, just maybe, Ray will find it.

John excuses himself moments before a commotion behind me wakes the sleepy spectators. Furious, the judge goes on a tangent about respecting everyone, including the Taylors' time. The crowd isn't listening. Fed up, the judge decides the court will recess until tomorrow.

Calvin is ushered out of the room before I can say goodbye. I reach out for him and grasp nothing but air. I long to wrap him in my arms, tell him everything will be okay, and have him believe me. Like I did when he fell off his bike when he was six.

John returns before I exit the courtroom and face the sprawling crowd of spectators and reporters. I wrap my arms around John's waist. Charlotte's purse hangs across my shoulder and she loops her arm through it. Together they are my bodyguards, protecting me front and back, as they push me through the crowd to our car. Randall and Ray stay behind to debrief with Calvin, before he's transported back to prison.

Reporters and citizens pummel me with questions about what it's like to raise a murderer. When I'm not being hit with questions, I'm hit with fruit, vegetables and unfinished takeaway coffee.

Charlotte's car acts as a shield for items people hadn't thrown before I took cover. "I can't believe they actually cut up tomatoes to throw at me." I say.

John helps me pick debris out of my hair. "On the bright side, we've seen what you'd look like as a red-head." John wipes as much juice as possible from my jacket. "Not sure I'm a fan, though." He winks at me. "On another note, we might need to talk to Ray about his speech delivery. There's no way the jury is going to keep their eyes open if he keeps drowning their ears with boredom."

"I'll talk to him," says Charlotte from the front seat. "John, did you see anything in the hallway on your way back?"

"Nothing that caught my attention. Mind you, I didn't realize there was something I should have been looking out for."

"Let's talk about this later. It's been a long day and I need to think," I say.

The hum of the engine, and rubber meeting asphalt, occupies the silent vehicle's passengers. John reaches for my hand, but I brush it away. We stare out of our respective windows.

Sheep graze on the hillsides, blissfully unaware the life of a passerby is falling apart. Birds swerve around each other and swoop down to kiss the water. Strands of seaweed dangle from their beaks when they bounce off the water's surface and back into the clouds.

If only I could scoop up Calvin and fly away to safety. But who would we be flying away from? Who is controlling the throttle on this gut-wrenching roller coaster? I need to find them and cut the cord to my past forever. I will not rest until I do. Otherwise, all will be lost.

I release all the air from my lungs, close my eyes and try to calm the scream that has lodged itself in my throat. I can't contain it once my feet hit the pebbles of my driveway and see that the word BITCH, in purple spray paint, has joined the repainted red MURDERER, on the front of my house.

"ARGH! These fucking people think they know what happened." I hurl stones at my house until John forces both of my arms to my sides.

"There's no point in adding a broken window to the mix. Let's go inside and see if we can figure out our next move," he says.

"Next move! It doesn't matter what we think we need to do, whoever's after me is already five steps ahead." I push John off of me and blast through my front door. The door to my liquor cabinet is the next victim of my anger.

Charlotte and John sit patiently in the living room until my boiling anger simmers. Charlotte's voice finally breaks the silence. "We were prepared for today to not be good, but that was bad."

"I don't have investigative experience like both of you, but how is it possible for the prosecutor to use manipulated photos as evidence?" John asks.

I still can't bring myself to speak, so I let Charlotte lead the conversation while I focus on draining and refilling my wine glass.

"They must have something that wasn't disclosed to me, and that Ray hasn't shared. We have an expert who can show the photos are manipulated, so the prosecutor has to have some way to call our theory into question. She mentioned the photos in her opening statement, so she has to be entering them as evidence. She's a smart woman and will not risk her career for this. Which leads me to these diary entries she mentioned. Was anyone aware of these?"

I shake my head, as does John.

"I'm going to call Randall. He should have received the full discovery package by now, but if not, I'll ask him to look out for those." Charlotte heads to the kitchen.

I lock eyes with John, whose face looks like a lost puppy. "Liv, don't take this the wrong way, but would you consider slowing down with the wine. That's four glasses since we got back."

Without wavering, I pour my fifth glass. "When your son admits to murdering someone, then you can tell me how much I can drink."

"I understand-"

"You understand nothing! I'm going to lose him completely. Not because of a phase teenagers go through, but full-on gone, and there's nothing you or Charlotte can do about it. We've lost." I say.

"We haven't lost," Charlotte replies.

"Really? Ray's shitty opening statement made him look like a fool. Evidence of Calvin's innocence is going to be used against us, and now Calvin wants to take a deal. What else would you call it?" I ask.

"A setback," John states.

"Fuck off, a setback. My son's a Goddamn murderer, John. He's William and there's nothing I can do about it." I hurl the empty wine bottle, and it shatters against the fireplace.

"He's not Wi-"

I cut John off. "Stop. You're not helping. In fact, you being here is making things worse."

"How?" he asks.

"Not only am I losing my son, but how long until you're gone?" I ask.

John rises from the couch and strolls towards me. "I'm not going to leave you."

"That's not what I meant." John's head tilts to the side. "The cancer, John. The Goddamn Cancer."

John hits an invisible wall and stops in his tracks.

"That's right, I know. And you kept it from me. You promised me you were fine. You lied to me. The one thing I asked you not to do. I can only wonder what else you're lying about?"

"I..." John's lost for words.

"Nothing to say? Figures. You should go. Charlotte and I took care of things last time. We can do the same this time." I say.

John lowers his voice. "What do you mean, handle things?"

"You know what I mean. Please, just go."

John gathers up his coat. "I don't want to go. I'm only leaving because you asked."

Arms crossed, I turn my back to him. I avoid the hurt I've caused, even if he deserves it. Footsteps echo into the distance. Silence follows the closure of my front door. I want to turn around and run to him. My feet stay firmly planted in place. The weakness of love is something I won't give in to. I don't have time for that. I need to focus on my son.

An engine roars and putters out moments later. John is gone.

The cool kitchen floor soothes my feet. "Why did you ask him to leave? We need him." Charlotte asks.

"Do we? What we need is to find Dr. Harrison, or whoever sent that letter. John doesn't have investigative experience. He'll just be in the way," I say.

"In the way? He was the one who figured out the photos were fake. What we both need is rest. And you need less wine."

"Why is everyone going on about my drinking? I'm fine. Besides, I won't be able to sleep, so let's get to work and tell me what Randall said," I say.

"I really think you're-"

"Don't mother me. Tell me what he said," I demand.

"It's not good," Charlotte warns.

"Why would any news today be good?" I slump into a chair. I'm exhausted, but won't let Charlotte in on that fact.

"There are pages and pages of electronic diary entries where Shaylynn worries about her safety and says Calvin is stalking her." She advises.

"Fuck! Show me." I'm not sure I can take any more evidence against my son, but I need to know what we are facing.

"Authorities took the website down," Charlotte advises.

"I'm talking to a Director at MI5, am I not? Get your people to access it," I demand.

"No," she says.

"No?" What was she playing at?

"I'm not showing this stuff to you. Truthfully, you're acting crazy and this will not help. I'll look into it, but I'm not causing you to spiral even further," Charlotte says.

"I can't spiral anymore. I'm at the fucking bottom."

"Exactly. Trust me, if there is anything there to help us, I will find it." Charlotte will not give in.

"Fine. Let's talk about Ray. What excuse did he provide for not telling the prosecutor about the doctored evidence?" I ask.

"Actually, he tried. Phone logs and emails show he reached out. Obviously, he didn't provide the specifics in the emails. You never know who is watching," Charlotte advises.

"I still don't trust him." I say.

"Me neither. That's why I have an agent surveilling him," she says.

"Good."

Charlotte pushes me out of the kitchen and away from the case of unopened wine. We sit on the couch and she holds me, as images of unrecognizable television characters dance across the flat screen.

My eyes focus on the picture of a little boy with a toothless grin, sitting on a silver bicycle, on the wall above the television. His future is slipping out of my hands like a colander trying to hold water. If I don't do something soon, the remnants of the boy I knew will be gone forever. Eaten up by the prison system. By his DNA. Replaced by a man I long to forget.

Chapter Thirty-Six

Calvin

I don't have to tell the other inmates to stay away from me. They keep a wide berth when I return. The guards even bring dinner to my cell, an act of kindness only shared when someone's too ill to walk. I can walk, but I wasn't about to complain. I just want to be alone.

The knots of nerves that inhabited my stomach earlier have made way for knots of hunger. I eat so fast, I can't taste the food. Which is probably best, as the chicken stew is never good.

Knuckles rap against my metal cell door. Marc leans over the threshold on one foot. "Sorry to disturb you, Calvin. I know you've had a, uh, strenuous day. But you have a visitor."

"I don't want to see my mother or my lawyers."

"It's neither of those. I think it's your grandfather?"

"Grandfather? I don't have a..." I trail off. Could it be M.? "Oh him. Okay."

I follow the familiar yellow line to the visitor center and there he is. Seated tall, hands folded in front of him on the table in the corner. His eyes dart between the occupants of the other tables. The voices of the full room will hide our conversation from nearby listeners.

M. was never much of a hugger, but he stands and pulls me close. I feel safe. We part and take seats opposite each other. The metal's warm. The last inhabitant's body heat has not yet faded.

"I'd apologize for not visiting sooner, but the truth is, I've heard that your lawyers are asking about me. Given my past, I thought it was best to stay away. I don't need to be involved in all of this. You understand."

M. used to be a member of a biker gang and got caught up in drug smuggling. He'd done his time, but he avoided the police as much as possible. They take one look at his record and can't help but let bias into their thoughts.

"Are they treating you alright in here?" M. asks.

"Yeah, they let me keep to myself."

"That's good. You don't need to be getting into any trouble while on trial. The prosecutor will use that against you and try to make the jury think you're a troublemaker. How did court go today? I saw it on the news. But reporters blow things out of proportion," M. says.

I have no cuticles to pick at, so I gnaw at my chewed up fingernails. "I don't want to talk about it."

"That good, huh? You know you can talk to me about anything?" he says.

"Yeah."

"That first lawyer of yours doesn't seem very smart, but I see you have two of them now?" M. asks.

"Yeah, looks like Mr. Bower can't be trusted, so Aunt Charlotte found another guy to make sure Mr. Bower doesn't fuck things up," I say.

"Really? Why don't you trust Mr. Bower?" he asks.

"Well, Mom and Charlotte don't trust him. I don't care anymore. There's no point. It's all over," I say.

"What leads you to believe that?" M. asks.

I make sure no one is listening, "Because I killed her," I whisper.

M. waits a beat before speaking. "Are you sure?"

"I remember doing it," I say.

M.'s mouth twitches upward. "Do you want to tell me what happened?" M. asks

"Not really. It's hard enough knowing I killed my best friend. I relive it enough. I'd prefer not to. But I have some questions. Why were you in the woods that night?"

M. hesitates and straightens his jacket. "I think you're mistaken. I wasn't in the forest. What leads you to believe that I was?"

"Because I saw you. Shaylynn ran right up to you. Then she and I passed out, or something. There was also someone dressed in black hanging around," I say.

"Are you sure you haven't imagined me into the scene? Maybe as some comfort since I'm the only one, next to Shaylynn, who's been there for you these past two years?" M. asks.

Why is he questioning me? "Yes, I'm sure. You wore a white dress shirt, grey pants, and the brown trench coat you always wear."

"I'm sorry, Calvin, but I wasn't wearing that outfit that night. I was out hiking most of the day and didn't get home until late. Even if you think you saw me, I wore a light blue shirt and brown shorts that day," he said.

"NO, YOU WEREN'T! Sorry. Sorry." Grease clings to my fingers after I run them through my hair.

"Everything okay over here?" a nearby guard asks.

"Everything's fine, thank you. It's been a stressful day for him. I'm sure you understand." M. answers.

The guard nods and backs away. He keeps his eyes on us for the rest of the conversation.

"Calvin, you're stressed, and it sounds like your memories might be mixing things up a bit. I wasn't there and I know nothing about a person in black. You should talk to a professional about it. They might help," he said.

"I'm supposed to be, but she hasn't come back. Mr. Bower can't find her and said we might as well wait until after the trial before finding someone new," I say.

"That sounds like a good plan. Focus on the trial and then, once you know what happens with that, take care of this other piece," M. says.

"I don't want to wait. I know what I saw, but I need the other memories to put everything that happened that night together. It's driving me crazy that I'm only seeing part of it," I say.

"I'm sure it's frustrating. Why don't I see if I can find this therapist of yours? What's her name?" M. asks.

"Fuck, I don't know." Why couldn't I remember something as simple as her name?

"That's okay. I have some friends who can check up on the visitor logs here. I'll find her," he says.

"Thank you." I feel sweat swim down my spine. "Look, I know you want me to call you M., to protect yourself and all that, but can't you tell me your name?" I ask.

M.'s eyes narrow and his lips roll in upon themselves. "I can't do that. Not yet."

"I could be in jail for the rest of my life and you won't tell me your goddamn name!" I whisper-yell.

Stern and steady, M. does not waver. "It is not the place or time to share that information. We have an agreement and I plan to stick to it. If you want to continue our relationship, that is the deal. Otherwise, I can walk out of here right now, not look for your therapist, and move on with my life. Your choice."

I'm torn. Ever since I killed Shaylynn, I didn't know what was right side up or upside down. Who to trust and who to be skeptical of. M.'s vagueness around who he is burrows a hole in my gut, and yet without him, I'd have never known the truth about my family. Why did everything have to be so hard?

"Can you at least tell me soon?" I ask.

"Once your mother is off the warpath. I don't need her coming after me for telling you the truth. How is she, by the way?" M. asks.

"Why do you want to know about her?" I ask.

"I just want to make sure she's taking care of you in all this, and not just focused on her new boyfriend." He says.

"Boyfriend? What boyfriend?" When did Mom find time for a boyfriend? I'm glad I'm her top priority.

"The Reverend or something? What's his name?" M. asks.

"John? Where'd you hear that?" I ask.

"Mrs. Olson."

"Of course, Mrs. Olson. So the whole town knows Mom is with Reverend John and once again I'm kept in the dark. Fuck her." The collar of my sweater is tight and itchy.

"She knows you're unhappy, and probably doesn't want to rub your nose in the fact she's happy." M. says.

"She doesn't seem happy. Although she is a master of hiding her feelings. Besides, Mom's focused on locating this mystery woman she thinks is after her. She's nuts is what she is," I say.

"Mystery woman?" M. asks.

"Yeah, she got this letter signed by someone who Aunt Charlotte says is dead. So now they're trying to figure out who would know to use the doctor's name to scare Mom. I don't think there is any happiness in doing that," I say.

"Maybe not."

"Mom was certain the doctor was you. Even showed me a picture of some woman outside a large manor house. She seemed a little disappointed when I told her I didn't recognize the woman. I told her you wouldn't do anything to hurt me and that you were a friend-"

"You told her about me?" M.'s teeth grind together.

"Yeah. I kinda had to. We were trying to find someone who could prove I didn't do this. And if you were there that night, then you could've helped. But it's too late for that now. The memories I have prove the truth," I say.

M.'s balled-up fingers are white, and his knuckles bright pink. "Did you tell her where I live?"

"I don't know where you live. Why does that matter?" I ask.

"A mother's wrath is not something I need on my doorstep. I need to go." M. towers over me, and I feel like a young child yearning for their protector to stay.

"Will you come back?" I need the one person I trusted close by.

"I can't promise anything. If your mother is looking for me, it might be best if I stay away until after the trial. Oh. I brought you this. It was the last one at the Cafe Shed. I wasn't sure guards would let you have it, but all they did was open the box. Enjoy." He hands me a small clear nondescript box. Inside is a vanilla and chocolate chip cupcake with cherry icing. My favourite.

"Thanks," I say.

Five long strides later, and he's gone. I turn towards my exit and almost collide with Marc. "Can't leave yet. You have another visitor," he says.

"I don't want to see anyone else. Can I please go back now?" I ask.

"Calvin?" The familiar voice pulls me around. The black shirt and white collar of the Sundays of my childhood stands before me.

"What are you doing here?" I ask.

"I need your help," John answers.

"You need my help?" What kind of help can a person behind bars provide?

"Yes. Shall we sit?" he asks.

I retake the seat I'd occupied moments ago. John takes up half the space M. had.

"Where'd you get the cupcake?" he asks.

"A friend," I say.

"What kind of friend?" John asks.

"I have friends, and that's all you need to know. Do you want my help, or should I leave?" I ask.

"Fine. But I'm going to circle back to that friend of yours," he says.

"Whatever." I glance at the clock and notice the end of visitation time is minutes away. I need to drag this conversation out long enough that I won't have to answer his questions about M.

"Your mom's not doing well," he states.

"And?"

"And I was hoping you could be a little nicer to her. Don't roll your eyes. She's a mess. Drinking too much, not sleeping, and being angry at everyone. She's you, but older," John says.

"Then I guess you know where I get it from," I say.

"Oh, I swear if I could slap you..."

"Would the good Reverend hit a kid? How loving of you. Maybe the people of Woodhaven will appreciate you more for taking on a murderer? Even if you are sleeping with his mother," I say.

"What did you just say?"

"You heard me. I know all about you and Mom. No thanks to her, either. Question for you: do you prey on broken women? I mean, you waited this long, so you must have a type, if you didn't want her before."

"That is uncalled for. I love your mother." John claws at the table to occupy his hands.

"Ha! Of course you do. And yet, when she reveals her true self to you, you come to me for help. If you think she's in trouble now, what will you do when you find out she's killed people? Oops, I guess I let that slip," I say.

"I'm aware of what your mother has done." The sucker punch I threw bounced back.

"Really? Well, don't people in your religion go to hell for killing people?" I ask.

"Everyone can receive God's forgiveness. And because of *you,* she is in hell. I'm sorry, I didn't mean... You know what? I did. And not because you think you killed someone. But because for the last two years, you've treated your mother like she's dirt. She's done everything she can to protect you. Even if you can't see it. As a child, you don't always get to know the minuscule details of why a mother makes a decision. Yes, not telling you about your father was wrong. She knows that. Despite the way you've treated her, she still loves you more than anything in this world. More than she loves herself. Because she's losing you, at a time when you both need each other most, she's taking out her anger on herself. She's falling apart at the seams and if you continue to disregard her, you'll be lucky to have a mother left at all. I will not be there for her forever. So you need to treat your mother with some love and respect."

Goosebumps dance under my sweater. I've never heard Reverend John speak like this, and I'm speechless.

He continues, "I don't want to load more onto you, given everything. But, to inspire you, you should know that I have cancer. Only a few people know, your mother being one of them. So she's carrying a lot right now."

"Shit." As much as I didn't like the idea of the Reverend shagging my mom, he didn't deserve to die.

"Yeah. And I wasn't the one who told her, so you know how that went over," John says.

"You're fucked," I say.

"Pretty much. She banished me from her house, so now it's her and Charlotte. I love Charlotte, but they are both too focused on your case to notice just how unraveled your mother is becoming. Which is not good for Olivia. I'm begging you, please be nicer to your mother." he says.

Many times growing up, Mom spent days in bed with little food, her own stench soaking trapped in the room by the unopened windows. If she fell that far, it would take a lot of work to pull her back up. Her son is a murderer, and once she realizes that, it'll push her over the edge. Push her to cling to her pillow as though it contains a lifesaving power she needs to squeeze out of it to survive. She needs to be free of all of this. Of me. "I'll try."

"Try hard. Now, let's talk about this friend of yours," John says.

Marc's booming voice fills the room. "Visitation hours are now over. All inmates rise and exit. Visitors remain seated until the inmates have left, and then you may proceed out the opposite door. Visitors, you may come back again tomorrow at eight a.m."

Saved by Marc. I follow orders and join the train of inmates back to the cell block.

I climb onto my bed and lean up against the plain white wall. The plastic container crinkles and cracks as I force it open. I bite into the Vanilla and chocolate chip cupcake. My tooth hits something hard. Cake sticks to my finger as I dig into the middle of the cupcake.

I find a piece of paper with something hard inside. I unfold the paper. Inside sits a silver razor blade and the note: *It's okay if it gets too hard.*

CHAPTER THIRTY-SEVEN

OLIVIA

The water in the glass on the coffee tables ripples from Charlotte's snores. After much reluctance to let me stay up, she falls asleep on the couch around two in the morning. Now I can get to work.

I take down all the photos from the wall in the dining room. Vacations to France. Calvin's second steps (I hadn't been quick enough with my phone at first). School photos. They all find a home in a stack on the floor in the corner.

I replace them with the articles I'd found under Calvin's floorboard and copies of the evidence Charlotte got. If there is a speck of white wall, I cover it. I stand back and take in my masterpiece. String maps where the police found each piece of evidence. I need to get into the mind of the killer. I'm trying hard not to believe it was Calvin and this will help prove it. He wouldn't take Shaylynn's life on his own.

"What is all this?" Charlotte rubs her eyes to hide her shock.

A small drop of blood balloons out of my finger where the teeth of the tape dispenser caught on my skin. "Shit, you scared me."

"And you're scaring me." Now beside me, Charlotte takes in the all-consuming wall of information.

"We need to look at it all again. This mystery friend of Calvin's is involved somehow, and we are missing the piece that links everything together."

"I have so many questions. But first, is there coffee?" Charlotte asks.

"You might need to make another pot." I advise.

"You've already drunk a pot of coffee? I worry about you sometimes." Cupboard doors collide with their frames and the smell of freshly brewed coffee trickles out of the kitchen.

"We should call John," Charlotte says over a steaming cup hugged close to her.

"No, we shouldn't," I reply.

"You're being petty," she says.

"He's dying and didn't tell me. One lie often leads to another and, given his family background, I can't deal with all of that stress on top of all of this," I say.

"He might not be dying. And he had a good reason not to tell you." Charlotte said.

"We're not having this conversation again." Time needs to be focused on Calvin, not John.

"I'm just say-"

The front door slams open. Charlotte reaches for a gun that isn't there. Our bodies shrink against the walls on either side of the dining room doorway. We wait for the intruder to appear. The sight of an arm is all it takes. Charlotte grabs their wrist, pulls them forward, kicks the back of their knees and cranks their arm behind them.

"Ouch! It's me!" John exclaims.

Charlotte twists him around. "You barge in here at dawn like the world's on fire. A simple knock would have sufficed. And be better for your arm." She loosens her grip, but keeps a hold of him.

"Sorry about that, the wind's howling out there and it ripped the door out of my hand. Anyway, I have news." John looks up at me. "Could you tell her to let me go?"

"I don't know. This is kind of fun," I say.

"Haha." John smiles.

I nod to Charlotte, and she releases him.

"Thank you. Now..." John turns around and his jaw drops. "What's all this?"

"Olivia did some arts and crafts while I was sleeping. Coffee? I have a feeling you'll need it." As quick as lightning, Charlotte brings John a sloshing cup of coffee.

"What am I looking at?" he asks.

"This will help us run through everything again. Something in here will help us find whoever's behind all this," I advise.

"I found him," John announces with gravitas.

"What?" Charlotte and I say in unison. "Why didn't you lead with that?" I ask.

"I was going to, until I came upon your serial killer wall. The guy goes by the name Travis Carter."

"How did you figure that out?" Charlotte asks.

"He visited Calvin yesterday," John says.

"You know this how?" I ask.

"After you kicked me out, I saw Calvin. I was trying to get him to see everything from your perspective, and maybe he would be nicer to you," John says.

"I don't need you to parent my son." What made him believe seeing my son would be okay? He was supposed to stay away, not get closer.

"Let's not focus on that right now. When I visited Calvin, he was holding a container with a cupcake in it. When I asked who it was from, he said it was a friend. He wouldn't tell me who, and visiting hours ended before I could get an answer. But how many friends are visiting Calvin in prison?" John asks.

"Their name would be on the visitor logs," Charlotte says.

"Exactly. I took a picture of the log as I was signing out. There was only one name I could find nothing online about."

"Travis Carter," I say.

"I grabbed a few dozen freshly-baked cinnamon rolls from Cooper's Bakery and went back to the prison. Patty was at the front desk."

"I hope you used her crush on you to your advantage," I say.

"She has a...Nevermind. Half a cinnamon roll later, Patty turns her computer screen so that I could see the identification that was scanned for the visitor. She wouldn't let me take a picture, but I jotted down the address. It's in Brampton." John says.

I wrap my arms around John so fast he doesn't have time to move his coffee cup out of the way. We're both covered and the scalding coffee burns, but I don't care. "Thank you!" I kiss the morning whiskers on his cheek. "We should go."

"Whoa. Hold up a minute. Let's think this through," Charlotte says.

"What is there to think about? We are running out of time and if he'll enter a prison to visit Calvin, he'll know we will follow up on that," I say.

"What if they are waiting for us? Let me at least arrange some backup," Charlotte says.

"Fine. But they better not take hours to get here," I say.

"I'll pull the guys watching Ray. They can meet us there in thirty minutes, I'm sure. In the meantime, you both need to change." Charlotte circles the dining room table. Quick glances bounce off my new wallpaper.

"I guess it's a good thing I didn't take my clothes with me last night," John jokes.

"Ah yes, we wouldn't want to miss out on you in your Ramones t-shirt." I try to hide my smile.

"What do you have against that band?" John asks.

"Nothing. The shirt is old and tattered, yet you still wear it," I say.

"It's comfortable," he replies.

"It's disgusting."

John and I meld back into our relationship as if last night's fight didn't happen. I'm still hurt that he kept the cancer a secret, but I would be a hypocrite if I didn't forgive him. He would have told me, eventually. I hope.

Charlotte's voice climbs the stairs. "Are you two coming, or are you going to shag first?"

"Do we have time?" John yells back to her.

I roll my eyes, stifle a laugh, and shuffle past him into the hallway. I need to get my hands on Calvin's *friend*.

Chapter Thirty-Eight

Stranger

My curtains dance in the cool evening breeze while it battles the heat from the sizzling fire. The flames aren't required, but the crackling and hissing of the logs are soothing after an eventful day. The woodsy taste of the whiskey also helps to take the edge off.

Court went well. Despite the lecture in the hallway from my son about my impromptu stroll through the courtroom. He wasn't wrong. I'd almost ruined our plans. I finish my drink in a large gulp, pour another, and I tell myself to never do that again. Not until everything's ready.

Which may need to be sooner, rather than later, now that Olivia knows Doctor Harrison wasn't the one to share all her secrets with Calvin. Typical teenager, tossing aside our agreement when it suits him. I'm glad I planned and brought Calvin a path of escape. A different road to revenge.

Calvin's mental anguish wraps around him like a cloak. Although I would enjoy every minute of Olivia's torment during a drawn-out trial, in the end, seeing her losing her son is my goal. If I need to expedite my schedule, so be it.

I rarely take pleasure in killing someone. It is just part of the job, but today my stomach flutters with excitement knowing I'll be the last person Olivia sees, before she takes her last breath, her eyes bulging out of her head. Much like they did when we tied her up, naked, in the stall block of Hammond Manor, and she saw the branding iron glow a bright yellow and orange in my hand.

169

I wish I was the one to mark her with an H, but Helen was the right one to do it. Helen was head of the family, and I was a simple man, with a self-imposed task to protect the mother of my child. I'd fallen in love with Helen when I was hired by the Hammonds at nineteen.

A thunderous slam of the front door retracts me from my thoughts. The walls vibrate in response.

Buck tosses his jacket onto the arm of a chair. The stopper of the whiskey decanter clangs upon exit and entry. Half of what remains ends up in Buck glass. Half of that is swallowed in one large gulp. "How could you visit him? Especially after what happened in the courtroom this afternoon."

"It'll be fine," I say.

"It's not fine. They scanned your identification, so your information is now on file. Charlotte is likely monitoring Calvin's visitors and now they've got your address. Where's your to-go bag?"

"In the front closet, but you're overreacting," I say.

"Even if I am, we need to be prepared. What were you thinking?"

"I was thinking my son is a failure, and hasn't ensured Calvin will be convicted of murder. The prosecutor may use all the evidence we gave them, but whoever you used to create those photos left a large opening for questions to be asked. And Olivia is asking those questions! I needed to clean up your mess."

"How is seeing Calvin cleaning anything up? There's surveillance video, for Christ's sake. You're so frustrating."

Buck's cough starts. Every time he gets upset, the cough starts.

"I set up an insurance policy. If we can't take Calvin away from Olivia, he will do it himself," I advise.

"Do you really think Calvin will kill himself?" he asks.

"He's convinced himself he killed Shaylynn. He'll do it to escape the nightmares and the weight of that idea alone."

"And today was the day you needed to do that?"

"You'll be thankful I did. Calvin remembers we were both in the forest. As you took care of the therapist, there's a window of time where he won't be working on retrieving the rest of his memories. I reassured him no one else was there, but the more he rummages around in his brain, the more likely he'll find the truth,"

"He believes we were there?"

"He remembers what I was wearing and another person in black. He doesn't know it was you. So that will keep Olivia guessing for a while. Do you understand why today's visit was beneficial?" I ask.

"I suppose. But you are still leaving this house. First, we need to tear down this ridiculous wall you put together. MI5 could be here any moment," Buck says.

"Leave it. Their skin will crawl with agony when they realize how close they got," I say.

"Then let's go." He said.

Faint blue lights bounce off the corner of the side mirror as we sink below the crest of the hill. A narrow escape. My heartbeat quickens and I look at my son, whose grip on the steering wheel makes his knuckles white.

"We should probably go over your testimony. It's going to have a big impact on what happens next," I say.

CHAPTER THIRTY-NINE

OLIVIA

John, Charlotte and I stand on the faded red and grey brick driveway of a cream brick house. The entryway extends from the main building, and white-trimmed windows take up the front. The entry is empty. Overall, the house is as unassuming as the ones on either side. Smoke floats out of the chimney.

The silencing of an engine draws our attention to the street. A large man in a dark suit steps out of a black Range Rover. Moments later, a smaller version of the man gets out of a similar vehicle.

Charlotte acknowledges them with a nod but doesn't introduce them. "Before we go in, what's the report on Ray?"

The men glance at each other. The smaller man wrinkles his forehead and, eyes on the larger man, nods towards Charlotte. A few silent rounds of 'you speak, no you speak,' later and the larger agent addresses Charlotte. "We lost him."

"How the fuck did that happen?" Charlotte asks.

He takes a few steps back. "I fell asleep."

"I'm sorry. Did you say you fell asleep? I think that's what I heard, but that would be impossible because then you'd be fired. Are you going to be fired, Carl?" Charlotte asks.

"Ma'am, I'm sorry. I dozed off for two minutes and when I woke, his car was gone." Carl replies.

"By two minutes, you mean?" Charlotte asks.

Carl's large neck shrivels into his collar. "Three hours."

"You've got to be kidding me! Do you realize how important this case is? Don't answer that, as obviously you don't, otherwise you wouldn't have curled up for nap time during your shift. After we're done here, you're going back to London. It'll give you an opportunity to find a nice template for a resignation letter."

Charlotte looks to the other man. His hands are folded in front, legs slightly apart. "Thank you for joining us on short notice, Steve. Did you get a picture of Calvin's visitor from the prison?"

"You're welcome, ma'am, and not yet. They are having issues extracting a still image from their system. Once we're done here, I'll head over," Steve answers.

"Not what I was hoping to learn, but I'm glad to have you here. Well, Carl here gets to go in first. Steve, take the back door, with Olivia. John, you wait here until we tell you. If you hear gunshots, run and call the police. I don't want you in a potential line of fire."

I pull out my gun from my jacket and follow the smaller man into the backyard. We don't hide our position. If anyone is home, they would have seen us by now. Will we still find who we are looking for?

The back door is unlocked, and creaks open. I can see over Steve's head with ease and in room after room, we encounter no resistance. After we check every room, Charlotte has Carl bring John into the living room. We all stare at a wall which could be a replica of the one in my dining room.

"Seems familiar?" Charlotte asks John.

"Wow. That's..." John's lost for words.

"Fucking creepy is what that is," Charlotte says and squeezes my hand, "and now you know why I don't want you to have a wall like this."

I take in what hangs before me. "He's been this close the whole time. Look at these photos. Hundreds of them from every year of Calvin's life. Have I had a conversation with him and not even known it?" I ask.

"I doubt it. He stayed in the shadows until he wanted you to know he was here. What I don't get is why he gave us the opportunity to find him. He'd have known identification would be required to visit Calvin. Why play that card when Calvin's trial has barely begun? If his goal is to hurt you, wouldn't he want to reveal himself after Calvin's conviction?" Charlotte asks.

"We need to go!" I run over Carl and head full-speed to the car.

"What's going on? Why are you panicking?" John yells behind me with Charlotte and the agents trailing him.

"We need to see Calvin. Charlotte, unlock the car!"

"I'll get you there, but you need to tell us what's happening," John says.

"The worst thing wouldn't be Calvin going to jail. The worst thing would be Calvin dead.

CHAPTER FORTY

CALVIN

The sharp silver blade twirls between my knuckles, like a twenty-pence piece used to. A couple of swift movements and everything will be over. Mom will be heartbroken for a while. But, this means the fear of me turning into my father, although a reality right now, will become a distant memory. She won't have to feign love to hide the hatred of a monster.

At least I'm not leaving her alone. She has Reverend John. He'll help her get over me. Even if he's sick, he didn't look like he was dying. Hell, he probably only told me that to make me feel guilty about how I've treated Mom.

M's note said, "*It's okay if it gets too hard.*" It's not that it's hard. More, I don't see any way else to find peace. Peace for everyone and peace for me.

This way, Shaylynn's parents will get justice. After what I did, they deserve justice, and I deserve to die.

How else can I ensure I don't kill again? The books I've been reading from the prison library point to both DNA and environmental factors contributing to a person's personality. Well, my DNA speaks for itself. My family ran a criminal enterprise with bodies buried all over their property. Bodies all over the world. Even my Mom has killed people. It's hopeless. I'm bound to take more lives. Even if I remain encased behind steel doors.

This is the only way.

My blood is warm. I find the trickle down my skin soothing.

Not long now.

CHAPTER FORTY-ONE

OLIVIA

The sheep that crawled by only days earlier, whip past today. My heart beats as fast as the speedometer. If Calvin's *friend* wanted to hurt me, all he needed to do was take Calvin away. For two years, Calvin was effectively gone, but the opportunity to come back to me was always present. If Calvin is dead, he can never come back. This would be the ultimate revenge.

"Can't you go any faster?" I ask.

"The needle is past the highest number on the gauge. This car can't go any faster," John says.

When we get to the prison, I jump out of the car before it comes to a complete stop. John yells after me, but the breeze carries his words away and not to my ears. It isn't important. Nothing is more important than my son.

"I need to see Calvin," I tell Patty. Her hair's pulled back into a tight bun and she looks quite pretty in the grey guard's uniform.

"Ma'am, breathe, and try to say that slower so I can understand you," Patty says.

"Patty, please, you know who I am. I need to see Calvin,"

"Right. Well, I just need to scan your identification-"

"I don't have time for this. My son is in danger. Let me in. Now!" I demand.

"Why do you think something might happen to your son?" Patty asks.

I walk past Patty's window and bang on the visitor's entrance door. "Can someone please help me?"

Patty yells after me. "Ms. Lyons, we won't be able to let you in, if you don't calm down."

"Calm down, you want me to calm down! John, Charlotte, you tell her what's happening. They won't let me in," I say.

The door I stand behind contains a glass window. All I see through it is another door. Solid, with no window. It leads into the hallway to the visitation area. I'm so close to Calvin and yet so far. Where is that adrenaline mothers get when they're terrified their child will die and can lift vehicles? No matter how hard I pull, push, or kick, the door doesn't budge. A loud buzz fills the entry.

"Finally," I say.

The Superintendent steps into the door frame before I can walk through. "Ms. Lyons, Reverend and?"

"Special Agent Charlotte Lewis."

"You three can follow me," he says.

He leads us down hallways I haven't seen before. "Where are we going? Isn't the visitor center back there?" I ask.

"I'm taking you to a private room where you'll be more comfortable," the Superintendent advises.

"More comfortable with what? What happened?" The hairs on my arms and the back of my neck stand tall.

The Superintendent opens a door into a cheap resemblance of a living room. "Have a seat."

"I don't want to have a seat. Take me to my son. Or, tell me what's going on!" I yell.

"If you'll-"

Charlotte steps in. "Thank you for letting us in. We believe Calvin may be in danger or hurt already. You bringing us into this room is confirming that suspicion, so you better tell us what's going on. Otherwise, you are going to experience a side of Olivia you would be safer not to."

"Okay. There's no easy way to say this. Calvin was found hurt in his cell. He'd slit his wrists."

Are his words real? Am I imagining them? I lose all sense of balance and collapse to the floor. John joins me on the floor and his shoulder muffles my screams.

The Superintendent and Charlotte huddle together and then he leaves, closing the door behind him. She crouches down beside us and rubs my back. "Hun, hey. Listen, Calvin's going to be okay."

"What?" I'm in a daze.

"Another inmate found him before Calvin lost too much blood. He was unconscious, but alive."

"Really?" I ask.

"He's in the infirmary and you can go visit him," Charlotte says.

John helps me to my feet. His eyes search mine, but I don't know what they're looking for. What more could he want from me in a moment where all that matters is seeing my son?

Calvin looks pale and fragile lying in the infirmary bed, intravenous lines and a heart monitor attached. He's only been in the hospital once, to have his tonsils taken out, and I was so nervous, back then, to let him out of my sight. Some unfathomable fear the doctors would exchange him for another child in the surgery room, irrational and yet gripping. Nothing like the heart-wrenching end-of-the-world fear that fills me now.

I brush Calvin's hair away from his face. He likes to keep it a little longer. A guard stands inside the door, staring at the wall across from him,which is the only way to provide us some privacy.

What I wouldn't give to climb into the bed and hold him. Protect him. Calvin's body takes up ninety-nine percent of the bed, as is. I'd crush him if I tried. Instead, I roll over a stool and put his hand in both of mine.

Calvin stirs and cracks open his eyes. "Mummy?"

"Yes, darling, it's me,"

"I'm sorry, Mummy,"

"It's okay. You did nothing wrong. Sleep now," I whisper.

"But M..."

I run my finger along Calvin's temple. "I know. Sleep. We can talk more later."

Calvin's eyes flutter as he walks through dreamland. Every so often, he squeezes my hand, unconscious of the fact I'm here in reality.

I'll sit beside Calvin until he awakens again. Then, I'll stay here until he's released from the infirmary. The opportunity for M. to finish what he started is lost. I'll go to jail myself, if it means keeping Calvin alive.

CHAPTER FORTY-TWO

OLIVIA

The commotion of the crowd lined up outside the courtroom drowns out the hollow sound of shoes pounding the marble floor of the courthouse. Beyond the regular metal detectors and bag scan upon entry, they have also set security up outside the courtroom. Everyone entering will have to show identification. The process moves at a tortuous pace.

Those testifying today sit on metal benches, under large windows, to the side of the line. I doubt they've been scrutinized like the spectators. If they had, Buck's relaxed smile would be nowhere in sight. Calvin's football teammates have their hands slapped away by mothers as they tug on their ties, suffocating from nerves. Buck tries to reassure the young men they will be fine. Mrs. Olson clutches the handle of her ruby handbag as she bounces in place.

Anyone reporting on this case has eaten up Mrs. Olson's desire to be heard. Today, she's going to have the undivided attention of a crowd scavenging for dirty little secrets. She will feed off of them, and they will feed off of her.

The courtroom's large oak doors are wide open, and create an ominous invitation to visitors. I give my new identification to one guard, who scans it with a thick black device with a small screen. A green border flashes around my picture on their device. Another guard pats every inch of my body except my groin, and then asks me to remove my shoes. Satisfied, I scan the boisterous room to identify where my foes are.

Charlotte stands in the front row of the gallery. She's having a very heated conversation with Ray Bower. I can't hear what is being said; however, her face grows darker shades of red, and her lips tighten, whenever he speaks. The turmoil of the conversation compounds the feeling of certainty today will serve me justice for Helen.

Olivia hasn't arrived yet. The Taylors sit in the opposite row of seats, behind the prosecutor's table. Despite my position in line outside the courtroom being somewhere in the middle, those before me have packed the courtroom like a train in rush hour. I maneuver my way through a sea of people and glare at a scrawny, beady-eyed young man seated in the far corner, as far away as possible from where Olivia is. For a few seconds, he tries to resist my non-verbal intimidation but relents and gives up his seat. The same dynamic scatters around the room. The meeker people curl their shoulders and arms in and make themselves as small as possible. The assertive crowd stands tall and tries to take up as much space as possible. The world eats the timid alive.

I don't have a magnificent view of where Olivia will sit, but reveling in her desperation is not my goal. I won't need to see her to feel the last ounce of hope being shattered as each piece of evidence buries Calvin deeper into Shaylynn's grave.

The crowd's voices ease into silence like the turn of a radio dial when Judge Parton is announced. The prosecution and defense teams take their seats. They have not brought in Calvin. Buck has said nothing, but I wonder if Calvin took my bait? It would explain why Olivia isn't here. He can't be dead, otherwise Charlotte wouldn't be here either. It's not ideal that Olivia is missing today's events; however, the result will still be the same--total annihilation of her life.

The judge announces, because of medical reasons, Calvin will not be present in court today; however, the trial will continue. Her authoritative voice muzzles the speculative crowd, and the prosecutor calls their first witness.

Teenager after teenager recounts incidents of Calvin's erratic behaviour, outbursts and fights. They share what they know about Shaylynn and her relationship with the accused. Ray Bower and Randall Tokarz both try to elicit favourable information from the boys, but, given the state of Calvin's recent relationship with them, it doesn't prove fruitful. One point to the prosecution.

The light wood panels of the witness box almost hide Mrs. Olson's tiny frame. She tries to hide her grin behind somber eyes and lips rolled in on themselves; however, as soon as she speaks, the edges of her mouth almost touch her ears. I'll give Mr. Tokarz credit for his cross-examination, he cuts Mrs. Olson down a peg or two, and ensures she does not trail from the facts into her "humble opinion". Observing the jury, it seems they appear torn if she is a nosy neighbour or a reliable source of information. Half of the jury either fiddles with their hair, taps their pencil on their notepad, or plays with their fingernails. The rest are enthralled. Half a point to the prosecutor and the defense.

It's the moment of truth for my plan. Buck is called into the courtroom. The crowd turns as though a beautiful bride is about to walk down the aisle. Nothing happens. The guard announces his name into the void of the hallway a second time.

Then I hear it.

"DOMINO!"

Two gray cylinders fly through the doorway and somersault in the air. One hits the back of a bench and ricochets into the aisle. The other jumps over the feet of the people standing against the wall behind me. Smoke hisses out of the end of the one I can see. It pops, and the smoke exudes faster. A wall of smoke is growing out of the ground. Frozen in confusion, the crowd becomes statues. I can still see Charlotte, so I can't move. I need to wait until I can hide in the smoke.

A loud explosion in the hall propels everyone to their feet, and the walls cannot contain their screams. Emergency alarms pierce my ears.

A herd of elephants jostles me out of my seat before I want to be. I turn up the collar of my brown trench coat and keep my head down, but my eyes up. The smoke thickens and I can only see the back of the person in front of me. Someone behind me grabs the back of my jacket and I elbow the unsuspecting person. They yelp and let go.

The occupants of all the courtrooms fill the hallway. Dust and more smoke create a screen of fear for those around me. Shattered glass crunches under foot. People shuffle, shoulder to shoulder.

I won't be able to hide in the crowd forever. I need out. People protest as I push them aside. Until one doesn't. A large man jostles with me and pins me to the wall with his forearm.

"Don't be an asshole!" He pushes himself off me and rejoins the crowd being herded to the exit. I clench my teeth and tell myself he isn't worth it. I need to focus on my safety.

A crash of glass breaking turns my attention behind me. That's when I see her. Dressed in a white suit, now spotted with dirt, her blond hair's pulled back. Her vivid violet eyes lock on mine and grow large. My gray hair and wrinkles are not a sufficient mask. Charlotte's hand touches her hip, and I know she's looking for the gun she couldn't bring into the building. The terrified screams of the crowd muffle Charlotte's yells of "Stop Him!"

I toss bodies aside as I navigate the sea of people in front of me until I'm breathing the exhaust-filled air of the parking lot. My head swivels as I try to find my car. Buck should have gotten away after he threw the smoke bombs. There's no time to worry about him now. We had an escape plan. He pulled the trigger and we will both follow through with our parts.

I jump into my car and peel out of my parking spot. Everyone else remains huddled outside the courthouse, curious as to the reason for their abrupt exit. Guards try to usher them away from the building.

Charlotte emerges from the group. Her figure is small in my rear-view mirror. She bolts towards me. I can feel her fury melt through the metal of my surroundings. There's a line of vehicles waiting to exit the parking lot. Charlotte gets closer. I swerve hard and jump the curb. Charlotte's fist pounds on the trunk of my car.

Her image diminishes into nothing once I get onto the main road. I take a deep breath and focus.

Time for Plan B.

Chapter Forty-Three

Olivia

The barred windows cast a checkerboard shadow on the slow and steady rise and fall of Calvin's chest. I move the invisible pieces around the board with my mind. Calvin and I played checkers for hours when he was little. Even before he understood the concept of the game. He just wanted to move the red and black pieces around. I miss the days when Calvin was full of innocence. When the world, to him, was a place where people didn't hurt each other, and a game of checkers was all that mattered.

The top of Calvin's hand is warm to my lips. I rub it like a rosary and pray that we will get through this. Together.

"You aren't crying again, are you?" Calvin yawns, and fumbles to sit up using his free hand. I let go of the other so he can get comfortable.

"A mother can cry over her child as much as she wants." I brush the hair out of his eyes and fluff the pillow behind him.

"It's a little embarrassing. I have a reputation to uphold here." He winks, and I wrap him in a hug.

"I love you," I say.

"I love you too, Mom." Calvin replies.

"Do you want me to see if they can bring you some food? You haven't eaten in a while."

"I'm fine." He twists the top of the infirmary sheets. "So, should we talk about this? Or..."

"I can start."

"Um. No, I'll go. I want to get this out." Calvin swallows deep and keeps his eyes on the sheets. "It's stupid, but I was so alone in my cell. A hundred people outside my door and yet solitary. I had no one to talk about this-"

"You can-"

"Mom, please let me finish."

"Sorry." My hands are rubbed dry from my time in the infirmary and scratch against my pants as I try to release the tension within me.

"I've been living under a mountain of hatred for myself. How can I live knowing I'm the reason Shaylynn is gone? I loved her, Mom." Tears fall down his cheeks. "Really loved her. Not just a high school crush. And I'm sure she loved me too. We were both too shy to say anything, but we knew." Calvin sips some water from the plastic cup on the table beside him, rests it on his lap and runs his finger around the top of it while he continues. "I wasn't a crazy stalker or anything like that lawyer lady said. And Shaylynn wasn't afraid of me. I don't understand why she would say that. We spent all of our time together. We were happy."

A slow stream of tears on my face mirrors Calvin's.

"So when I found that blade in my cupcake, I figured if I wasn't here anymore, it would be better for everyone. The town would stop harassing you. You wouldn't have to spend the rest of your life visiting me in prison. You'd blame yourself for my imprisonment. Even if you think you could handle it, you'd fall apart. The self-blame would eat away at you until you spent every day in bed, like when I was younger. Please believe me when I say what I did wasn't your fault. I also hoped maybe the Taylors would be happy I was dead. A life for a life, you know. It wouldn't have brought Shaylynn back, but it's the only apology that would be good enough." Calvin said.

I can't hold back anymore. Every tear inside my body comes out. "Oh, baby. I'm so sorry you have to go through all of this. You say none of this is my fault, but if I'd been honest with you, we might not be sitting here. That is a burden I'll carry for the rest of my life. Whether you think I should or not.

I continue, "You are not alone in fighting your demons. We all have them. One of mine is knowing that I almost took away life with you before it even began. I questioned whether I was fit to be a mother with all the trauma that led to your creation. I feared if I brought you into that family I would be a horrible mother. Especially knowing your father, or another member of his family's network, would kill me the moment you were born."

"What stopped you?" Calvin asks.

"Charlotte. I had a piece of broken mirror clenched in my hand and was ready to end it all when she walked in. There's not a day I don't think about that moment, staring at my reflection in the small piece of mirror, planning to leave this world behind. Even with the battle we've been fighting these last couple of years, I wouldn't change anything."

"Even though I became who you feared most?" Calvin asks.

"You're not your father. William only ever thought about himself and, with each decision, made sure he was the benefactor. He was calculated and cold. He never would have sacrificed himself to make other people happy." I cup Calvin's face in my hands and kiss his forehead. "I'm so sorry my fear of William consumed me so much I couldn't see past it. From now on, I will see you as you are. And I'll tell you everything about my past and your father. No holding back."

"I'm not sure I want to hear more right now. I'm sorry my father hurt you."

"Thank you."

He smiles and squeezes my hand. "There are some things about the night I killed Shaylynn that you should know. Please don't get upset that I didn't tell you. I was mad at you and-"

"I understand and I won't get mad."

"I remember that M., or whatever his name is, was in the forest." Calvin reveals.

"What?" My chest constricts and clutches my heart. The base of my skull warns me a headache is imminent.

"He told me he wasn't there, but I'm positive he was. Someone else was there too, but I can't figure out who. I can't see a face."

"I swear I will-" I squeeze Calvin's hand tight.

"You said you wouldn't get mad."

I loosen my grip. "I'm not mad at you, honey. I'm mad at him for using you to get to me. For manipulating you into this whole mess. It's been about me the entire time and you're a casualty in a cruel family game."

"I think the other person might be a man. I'm sure he whispered 'Now another.'"

"What does that mean?" I ask.

"No clue." He answers.

I restrain myself from fleeing the room as Calvin recounts what he remembers. I will hunt down this M. person and make him pay for the destruction he has caused.

The infirmary door smashes open. Three guards run in with the Superintendent. The guards go straight for Calvin and yank the cords from the machines and hang them over the back of the upright portion of the bed.

"Mom? What's happening?" I barricade Calvin's bed with my body. It will not be moving before I have answers.

"Ms. Lyons, we need to move your son back to a cell," the Superintendent says.

"Why?" I ask.

"For his own protection." The guards look to the Superintendent for their orders.

"Why does he need protection? And how is moving him back to his cell where he... How is that going to help anything?" I ask.

"We'll put him in a different cell. But we are locking this place down and will have guards outside his door." He peels me away from the bed.

"What. The. Hell. Is. Going. On?" I scream.

Charlotte walks into the room, gun in her hand and focused. "Olivia, I'll explain in the car, but you need to let them take Calvin. He'll be fine."

"Are you sure? I almost lost him after he was born because you had a hard time finding William."

My words bounce off of her. "Trust me."

"I'm sorry, I didn't mean-"

"It's fine. You're stressed. Local police are scrambling to locate Caldwell, but I fear they are more worried about covering their collective asses for when the media finds they were colluding with him against Calvin, than they are actually trying to find him," Charlotte says.

Her words transform into a mystic ghost before me. The tall, broad-shouldered man, whose eyes flicker like flames as they bore holes into me. At Hammond Manor, he was always watching me and never trusted me. Helen's most loyal soldier never let go.

"How did we not realize Caldwell was so close this whole time? And what do the police have to do with all of this?" I ask.

"Say goodbye and we can walk and talk," Charlotte says.

I embrace Calvin and squeeze so hard he gasps for air. Our eyes reflect the fear we will never see each other again. When Calvin's bed disappears around a corner, and I can no longer hear the wheels, I follow Charlotte in the opposite direction. I try to keep up with her brisk pace.

"Answers, please." I demand.

"Caldwell's been getting information from someone in the Woodhaven police department," Charlotte says.

CHAPTER FORTY-FOUR

OLIVIA

The bright sunny sky does not match the downcast mood in Charlotte's car. Everything outside the vehicle's a blur. My seatbelt strangles me as I squirm in my seat, trying to navigate what I hear.

"Caldwell's been working with a Woodhaven police officer? How the fuck did we not know that?" I ask.

"Nothing pointed to any concerns. I read their file a hundred times and I found nothing that led back to him. It looks like he used a burner phone and tipped them off on where to find evidence," Charlotte replies.

"You mean where he planted evidence to convict my son? Calvin didn't kill Shaylynn. Caldwell only wants Calvin to think he did. Oh, thank God!"

"Now you need to explain." Car horns outside blare as Charlotte weaves through traffic.

"Calvin's dreams. Caldwell was there that night in the forest. He gave him and Shaylynn something to drink. Calvin remembers Shaylynn passing out first and then he did. There was also a man dressed from head to toe in black. He never saw a face but swore it was a man's voice,"

"Another man?" Charlotte asks.

"Yes."

"But the officer helping Caldwell is a woman. Officer Cole."

"What? No, Calvin clearly remembers the man's low voice saying, 'now another,'"

"Another what?"

"I don't know. That's not the point. Are you sure it's Officer Cole?"

"She came forward after what happened at the courthouse today," Charlotte says.

"I'm going to need you to elaborate, given I wasn't there."

"Sorry, everything's moving so fast. Smoke bombs went off in the courtroom, followed by an explosion in the hallway, which meant everyone had to evacuate the courthouse. Who do I see across the crowd as the dust and smoke settle? Caldwell. I'd recognize him anywhere."

I close my eyes and try to steady the spinning around me. Charlotte continues, "The crowd was as thick as molasses, but I pushed through. I got as close as punching his car, but he got away."

"How the hell did Officer Cole get smoke bombs into a courtroom?" I ask.

"She said that wasn't her. The explosion happened right outside our courtroom. Preliminary reports show the bomb wasn't on a timer, so the person had to have been in the hallway. Officer Cole was in the courtroom."

"That means there is a third person helping Caldwell." My lungs deflate. "What else has Officer Cole shared?"

"She thought she was helping to catch a murderer. But after today, she realizes she's been helping one get away with it. She went straight to her Chief Inspector and told him everything. Caldwell would text her where to find evidence, like Calvin's stash under the floorboard and Shaylynn's on-line diary. Which is probably fake. The computer techs are working on it, but the IP address of the posts does not come from Shaylynn's house or the phone towers in town. The diary posts were dated prior to Shaylynn's death. However, the actual dates in the metadata say they were created after her death." Charlotte explains.

"How could Officer Cole think what she was doing was okay? And not suspicious?" I ask.

"It's a big case and people want to do right by the Taylor family."

"By blindly following random text messages?"

191

"You know how heavy the pressure can be. I think Officer Cole just got caught up in something she didn't understand."

"So if she's not the other person in the forest, or the one with the bombs, who is?"

"Your guess is as good as mine. The courthouse CCTV got interrupted and was down for the entire incident," Charlotte reveals.

"Convenient," I say.

"Yeah. We are still trying to determine how that happened."

"Charlotte, all your unknowns are killing me. You have access to the world's information and yet we have nothing on where Caldwell is or who else is helping him. My son's life is on the line here!" This moment mimics the anxiety and helplessness I felt trying to find Claire. I'm so close and yet any moment I could learn I'm too late.

"It's frustrating, but all of my agents are on this. We will find them. I promise," Charlotte says.

"I need this to be over, and I need Calvin back home," I say.

"And you'll get that. Soon," she encourages.

"Wait, where's John?"

"At the police station. He slipped out of the courtroom during Mrs. Olson's long-winded testimony. He'd left his phone so the guards wouldn't have to inspect it again when he came back. Then chaos ensued, and I couldn't find him in the crowd. Someone finally let him borrow their phone so he could tell me he was okay. I knew about Officer Cole by then, so I asked him to monitor things at the police station."

I push away the gnawing in the middle of my gut that's eating away at my trust in John. I'm being paranoid. Charlotte's cell phone rings and connects to the car's bluetooth receiver. "This is Agent Lewis. You are on speaker and Olivia Lyons is present."

"Agent, this is Chief Inspector Reacher. We finished talking to Officer Cole and you need to get to Reverend John's place," he says.

Charlotte and I look at each other. My gut screams, but only I can hear it. Charlotte asks, "Why?"

"I can't send my guys in there. Conflict of interest and the rest of the mess this case has caused. I need you to handle it correctly," he says.

"Handle what correctly?" I blurt.

"Bringing in Caldwell's son," he advises.

CHAPTER FORTY-FIVE

STRANGER

My head almost collides with the steering wheel when I slam on the brakes outside of a small cabin tucked along the cliffs. I whip around and make sure no one has followed me. Only then do I breathe.

I can taste the salt in the air. I hide my car underneath a tarp in a rundown barn off to the side of the cabin. We'll be taking Buck's car to the shipyard, and I don't want mine to be found before we can get out of the country. I look up to the sky, stretch out my arms and bask in the birds chirping. A moment of peace before I prepare the cabin for visitors.

The open-concept kitchen and living area take up the major portion of the small square place. The previous owners added a small bathroom and bedroom after they built it. Minimal furniture sits in the cabin. I have never intended the place to be for living, just a stop-over as needed, and Olivia and Charlotte's ultimate resting place.

After scarfing down some baked beans and bread, I get to work. I double-check the locks on the wheels of metal tables in the center of the bedroom. I line up my knives from largest to smallest, the bottom of every handle lined up with the handle beside it. The gas can is full. I position it away from the wood-burning fireplace.

I hesitate to put more wood in the stove and ignite the fire again. What is taking Buck so long? Reverting to Plan B meant we had a small window of time to get the women here, kill them, and flee. Each minute that passes takes away from the time I have to enact as much pain as possible before they draw their last breath. My love for Helen and what our son could have been twists the anger in my stomach as it yearns to get revenge.

I turn on my cell phone. No messages and no service. I turn it back off. The battery needs to be saved.

I can't stay cooped-up in this place. From the cliffs, I'll be able to hear any vehicle that drives the gravel entry.

Thin white clouds fade into the blue sky, a soft canopy for the birds to fly through. Waves crash along the rocks below. Trees in the distance rustle in the soft wind. All of these sounds are working in perfect harmony to create a symphony in nature. Each drop of water, leaf and chirp creates its own melodic call.

I try to get lost in nature's song and free myself from the list of tasks I keep running over in my mind. It doesn't work. I am pulled to do something with my hands. The yellow handle of an axe sticking out of a tree stump catches my attention.

Log after log is split. My shoulders burn. The stack on my right gets smaller as the one on my left enlarges.

If Buck doesn't get here soon, I'll have to find Olivia myself. I'm not wasting all my years of work.

Stones pelt metal.

Finally.

I keep the axe with me. Just in case.

A vehicle door slams.

I move up the side of the house and peer around the corner.

"Well, you're not my son," I say.

Chapter Forty-Six

Calvin

The longer I'm locked in this cell, the crazier I go. The two guards outside my new residence won't tell me what's happening. They keep saying I don't need to worry about it. Really? If I didn't have to worry, I'd still be in the infirmary.

In an act of kindness, they have left the food slot open so I can at least see out of my cell. I can see a portion of the common area and four of the cells on the opposite side. None of them have guards. Curious eyes peer out of their slots. Other inmates yell and bang on their doors in protest to the lockdown.

I pace in circles and drag my hand along the wall behind me, the ripple of the concrete like braille. My hand stops and I press my palm against the cool wall. The alcohol Shaylynn and I drank had to have been spiked with something. That's why we passed out. What if I wasn't supposed to remember anything that happened?

Now that my memories are revealing themselves, someone who doesn't want me to recall how Shaylynn died is after me. Mom was right. It has to be M., or rather this Caldwell person Charlotte mentioned. Why else would he give me that razor or get angry when I insisted he was in the forest?

My chest hurts when I think about Shaylynn. If she was here, she'd know what to do. How to figure this all out. She begged me to stop visiting M., damn it, Caldwell, his name's not M. She said she felt like snakes were swimming in her stomach when she was around him. Why didn't I listen?

My stitches itch. I rub them, but it doesn't help. I tear off the gauze. The black stitches along both arms look like the planks of a railway. I didn't feel the blade pierce my skin, but looking at the damage I caused to myself, I can now.

Trying not to think about the pain, I replay the events in the forest over in my mind. Shaylynn's black eyes and hair snakes must be the spiked drink playing tricks on me. I'm not going crazy, even if it feels like I am. Nothing new is revealed from my memories. I have to be missing something. I'll replay it again. Nothing stands out. Again.

Wait.

Shaylynn didn't run to Caldwell. She collides with him. We were racing to see who could get out of the forest first. After the collision, Caldwell grabs Shaylynn's wrist and whispers something in her ear. Then, the person in black comes up behind me and grabs my shoulders. They push me forward.

Caldwell pries Shaylynn's mouth open, and the liquid from the flask is forced down her throat. Then she falls to the ground. I wait for myself to be forced to drink, but I don't. I just fall. And then I'm awake beside Shaylynn's body.

Fuck!

I pound my head with my fists. Remember you, idiot!

I replay it again.

I focus on the person in black. They're tall. Not fat, but not skinny either. They seem familiar but I don't know how. I'm about to stab Shaylynn. My brain fights back. It wants to hide the memory. I need to remember. She screams. I look down and my hand is around the knife inside of her.

The figure in black says, "Now another." I look over.

The moonlight spotlights his eyes.

I come out of my memory, out of breath and paralyzed in fear for my mother.

CHAPTER FORTY-SEVEN

OLIVIA

Charlotte's grip on the steering wheel tightens. Her knuckles go white. Jaw clenched, she stares at the road ahead. My door handle feels my rage as the Chief Inspector brings us up to speed. "Miles Caldwell and Helen Hammond had a son forty-six years ago. They put names other than their own on the Entry of Birth. With Officer Cole's version of events, we contacted your office, Charlotte, and had them email us copies of all the photos in Caldwell's house. We found some old photos of Caldwell and his son. We'd recognize those eyes anywhere," he says.

We make it halfway through a tunnel and the call cuts out. "Shit." Charlotte presses some buttons on the dash, but couldn't get the call to go through. She's messed up something with the dash as she can't seem to make any call. "Can you figure out how to take my phone off bluetooth, put it on speaker, and call Agent Steve Hamm?"

"Who?" I ask.

"The short agent that helped search Caldwell's home. His number's in my phone. Try him," she says.

I dial and place the phone in a cup holder. My knees bounce with every ring. Finally, Steve picks up. "Charlotte?"

"Steve, great. Where are you?" Charlotte asks.

"Outside the Reverend's house," Steve answers.

"Perfect. What's happening?" Charlotte asks.

"Police have the place surrounded, and it looks like one person is inside. They closed all the curtains once the first cars arrived. Everyone is holding their positions until you get here," he reports.

"Good. Where is the Chief?" Charlotte asks.

"I don't think he's here. One sec I'll ask. Nope, they say he's at the station," Steve says.

"What the fuck is he doing there? You know what? It doesn't matter. We drove through a Goddamn tunnel and lost his call. You'd think people would have figured out how to get cell service through a tunnel by now," Charlotte seethes.

"Ma'am, I think it is the thickness of the cement or stone-"

"I don't care about how tunnels are constructed, Steve. I need the name of the person who is in that house. Ask the people around you," Charlotte orders.

"Right, one moment." A faint 'I don't know' creeps through the phone before it is muffled. Finally, Steve comes back on. "You will not like the answer," Steve reports.

"Because it's my friend or because no one has any idea who's in there?" Charlotte asks.

"The latter."

"Fucking sheep, all of them. They surround a house without knowing who they're looking for. How is that even possible? No wonder Caldwell could infiltrate their office. No one knows what the fuck they are doing!" Charlotte's face turns red, and invisible smoke pours out of her ears.

"They were just told to arrest anyone who walks out," Steve advises.

"Once I'm done with whoever's in that house, the Chief Inspector and I are going to have a little chat. We're a few minutes away. Please try to get me something before I get there," Charlotte says.

"Yes-" Charlotte hangs up before Steve can finish.

"I'm such an idiot," I say.

"No, you're not. There's still a chance it's not John," Charlotte encourages.

"Really? He wasn't beside you in the courtroom when the bombs went off. He conveniently doesn't have his phone, and he keeps secrets from me. I bet that the Entry of Birth I found was planted just to put me on edge," I say.

"My gut is telling me it's not him," Charlotte says.

"My gut tells me it is. So, unless you have something more interesting than he's always been a nice guy, I can't see how it's not him. He's been close to my son his whole life, close to the case, and around every time we found something that could help Calvin. He would know when to switch tactics. No one hates this more than me, but there's no other explanation," I say.

We pull up behind the police car blocking the driveway to John's house. The stone front is no longer inviting.

"There's a gun in the glove compartment. Only use it for defense. You are not a cop anymore, and I cannot have you discharging a weapon unless justified. Especially a service weapon registered to me," Charlotte advises.

"I think killing the people involved in taking my son away is justified."

"We will deal with that after. For now, we need this person to tell us where Caldwell is."

"Just say John. You need John to tell you where his father is."

"I won't say it until I see his face. Let's go," Charlotte says.

Charlotte and I are buckled into bullet-proof vests as she conducts a meeting with the crowd on the front lawn. Everyone else is to provide cover while she and I go in. She wants me to wait outside, but I don't protest long before she acquiesces. Steve will enter from the rear of the house. Charlotte and I stand on either side of the front door. Her hand rests on the doorknob. She mouths one, two, three and pushes the door open.

Living room. Clear. Dining room. Clear. Steve meets us in the hallway after clearing the kitchen. A rustling noise from the office draws our attention. Steve slowly turns the doorknob, then flings open the door. Charlotte bursts inside, followed by Steve and then me.

My breath is trapped in my throat. I lock eyes with the man in black, standing beside a raging fire in the stone fireplace.

"There's no need for guns, is there? I'm standing here peacefully."

"I think we'll keep our guns out. Steve, check him," Charlotte orders.

The figure in black lifts his arms and spreads his legs. Steve pats him down and advises, "He's clean."

"Good. Give us the room," Charlotte orders.

"Ma'am?" Steve queries.

"I said give us the room. Report back to the officer in charge outside that we have him and wait for further instruction," Charlotte states.

"And who am I reporting we have found, Ma'am?" Steve asks.

"Daniel Whitaker," Charlotte replies.

Chapter Forty-Eight

Olivia

The fire casts an ominous shadow over DI Whitaker's face. The office walls close in on me and I lean against the door frame to stay upright. "You're Caldwell's son?" I ask, trying not to let my finger slip and pull the trigger.

"Of all the small towns you flee to after your torturous time with the Hammonds, you pick mine. Fate really doesn't like you." DI Whitaker coughs and steps forward.

"Don't move," Charlotte yells. The barrel of her gun points to the middle of his chest.

"Oops. Sorry." He winks. He tested his boundaries and found there were none. "I wanted to kill you, Olivia, as soon as I found out you were in Woodhaven. You're the reason my mother is dead and my father's been in hiding all these years. Did you know I was supposed to take over the Hammond Empire? Not William. Me. You destroyed that possibility for me. You can count yourself lucky you had the eighteen years we gave you. That all changes today."

"You don't honestly think you have power here, do you? Where's your father?" Charlotte asks.

"Oh come now, don't you want to learn what happened to Shaylynn first? It's a fantastic story. I think you'll like it," DI Whitaker says.

"Can I please shoot him?" I ask. "Just in the kneecap. Nowhere vital. Not yet."

"It's tempting, but no. However, you, sir, have five minutes before I let her shoot you. So you better talk fast," Charlotte says.

"But then I'll need to leave out all the juicy pieces," DI Whitaker says.

"TALK NOW!" Charlotte yells.

"Fine. But may I sit?" DI Whitaker asks.

"Yes. Wait." Charlotte wheels over the desk chair. "Here."

"Think I hid something under a couch cushion, do you? Smart lady," DI Whitaker says.

Charlotte searches the couch, finds a gun and tucks it in the waist of her pants. DI Whitaker continues, "Right, Shaylynn. Such a beautiful girl. Too bad she was the one who got close to Calvin. In the end, it didn't matter which girl, or boy, took Calvin's fancy. For our plan to succeed, they would have ended up dead. Oh Olivia, your family really attracts death, doesn't it? How does that make you feel?" Phlegm loosens from DI Whitaker's lungs.

"I've changed my mind. Forget the knee. I have a fondness for shooting men in the penis." I take aim.

"Okay. Don't lose your head. Haha. See what I did there?" DI Whitaker says.

"You're stalling. Talk," Charlotte replies.

"I wonder why I want to stall?" DI Whitaker massages his chin.

"Calvin's safe. No one can get to him," I say.

"Oh, we're not going after Calvin today," DI Whitaker says "Our focus is on you two."

"And now you have us," Charlotte says. "The explosion today at the courthouse. That was you?"

"I was about to testify when a reporter asked me how I was going to explain my fingerprint on the tip of the murder weapon. If she knew it was there, then Mr. Bower and Mr. Tokarz are aware. I couldn't stand in that witness box. I would have been arrested before I got out of it. Being friends with the security guards and carrying a Woodhaven Police badge has its perks. No search upon entry. Father and I had a plan of escape if we needed it. Today we did," DI Whitaker says.

"The word domino was some sort of code?" Charlotte asks.

"Yes. A warning before the smoke bombs went off. But enough about me. Olivia, where's your boyfriend? Isn't he like your third musketeer?" DI Whitaker asks.

I lunge at DI Whitaker. I knock him, and the chair, to the floor. He rolls on top of me, but I hit him so hard with my gun, he falls to the ground beside me. Charlotte stands above us, gun pointed at DI Whitaker, while I climb on his stomach. His arms pinned with my legs. "Where is John?" I ask.

"Hmmm. I don't quite remember," DI Whitaker says.

SMACK. My gun meets his temple. "Where is John?" I ask again. DI Whitaker smirks. WHACK. Blood pours from his nose and gums. I cock the gun and press it into his shoulder. "You have ten seconds."

"I like this game. Shall we count together? Ten. Nine. Eight..."

BANG

"Fuck! That's not playing fair," DI Whitaker says.

I put all of my weight on DI Whitaker's injured shoulder and push myself off of him. Steve runs into the room.

"We're fine," Charlotte says, "stay outside the door."

Steve yells down the hall for people to hold back. He remains positioned in the doorway.

"This is useless. Can't I just kill him? We can find John and Caldwell another way," I say.

"Not yet. Sit up," Charlotte orders.

DI Whitaker pushes himself up again into the brown wall. Blood smears a trail in his wake.

Charlotte continues. "You like to tell stories, which I'm sure are very good ones. But we don't have time for that. So, instead, you are going to answer my questions or I might let Steve play with you for a bit. He might be small, but, man, does he know how to get people to talk. He has saved this country from threats no one has ever heard of. All with a couple of tweezers, some knives and a clamp. As much as I'd love to give Olivia the chance to kill you with a simple bullet, that's too good for you. Are you ready to talk?"

"You're no fun. I suppose you can ask your questions. But leave father to last. I have to at least try to give him time to get away. What kind of son would I be if- OUCH!" DI Whitaker yells.

The nozzle of Charlotte's gun presses into the bullet hole. "Who killed Shaylynn?"

A grin reserved for The Grinch spreads across his face. "Calvin."

"He'd never do that," I say.

"With a little help, he would." DI Whiateker's eyes gleam with excitement.

"Who helped him?" Charlotte asks.

"Father and I. Well, mostly me. Calvin was so drugged he could barely hold the knife. I had to guide his hand each time."

"You made my son kill Shaylynn. You bastard! I'll kill-"

Charlotte steps in front of me, hugs me, and whispers, "Calm down. We need information."

"Fine." My eyes never leave DI Whitaker's.

Charlotte turns back to DI Whitaker. A pool of blood forms around him and his face is pale. "What did you use to knock out the kids?"

"A little homemade concoction that took ten years to perfect. It keeps a person awake enough to move, yet still compliant with instructions. The limbs go a little numb at first, but after a few moments you can walk around, use your arms, stab someone. The usual things," DI Whitaker says.

"So, the toxicology report was altered?" Charlotte asks.

"See, I said you were smart." DI Whitaker's cough is getting worse.

"Why are you at John's?" I ask.

"Everyone knows he has some cash kept aside for emergencies. But the bastard moved it. It's not in the safe. Or anywhere in this house," DI Whitaker says.

"Where is your father?" Charlotte repeats.

"With John," DI Whitaker says.

"Why is he with John?" I ask. My heart should be used to the pain of trepidation, but it aches just the same.

"I sent him there. I thought I would let Father play with him for a while, rather than me killing him here. Not long after he left, the police showed up.

It's sad I'll miss out on all the fun with the two of you, though. At least Father will get his revenge. That's what matters," DI Whitaker says.

Enough is enough. I push past Charlotte and the barrel of my gun kisses his forehead. "Address now or you die."

"I'm gonna die anyway. If not from blood loss, the cancer will take me soon enough. John and I have something in common there. Except my cancer's terminal. So you'd really be doing me a favour," DI Whitaker says.

Damn him! I will not be doing him any favours. "Charlotte, let Steve go at him. I have another idea. You still have John's phone, right?"

"Yeah. In the car." She answers.

"Then we can find him. Teenagers kept stealing his car and leaving it all over town or outside of it. So when he got a new car, he made sure the navigation system included a GPS tracker. Since it's built right into the car, it only dies if the car battery does. It reports to an app on his phone." I march past Steve and the plethora of officers outside. In the passenger seat I pull out John's phone from the console in between the front seats. It asks for a numerical password.

Charlotte gets in the driver's seat. "Did you get in?"

I type 0514. The day I moved to Woodhaven. "I'm in." I find the app. Charlotte and I hold our breath while it loads.

A blue dot flashes.

"Thank God, he's not far." I type the longitude and latitude from the app into Charlotte's GPS.

I focus on the blue dot. Each rapid pulse matches my heart beat. John, we'll be there soon. Please hold on a little longer.

CHAPTER FORTY-NINE

STRANGER

The rickety porch creaks as Reverend John turns around. A nine millimeter handgun raises to my eye level. The cool breeze does not stop the sweat from covering Reverend John's face. His hands shake as he stares down the barrel of the gun.

"How nice to see you, Reverend John." I was not expecting this visitor; however, it is a pleasant surprise. Someone to fill my time with, while I wait for Buck. My heart rate and breath remain calm as I survey the scene. If I can get the Reverend into the house, I'll have a wonderful surprise for Olivia when she arrives.

"You need to come with me." Reverend John's voice quivers like his hands.

"Do I?" I lean against the corner of the house, the axe out of Reverend John's view. "I think it might be better if we talk inside."

"We don't need to talk. Now head towards my car."

"And if I don't? Are you really going to shoot me, Reverend? That wouldn't be very Christian of you."

"After what you have done, I'm very tempted."

"Have you ever shot a gun before? I'm betting not. I could attack you, and you wouldn't be able to hurt me." Reverend John appears confused. "The safety on the side of your gun needs to be switched off."

Without lowering his arms, Reverend John glances at the safety and it clicks. His fear creates a fog around us and I know he won't shoot me.

"Let's go," he says.

"Once you get me in your car, then what? I'll attack you from the front or backseat and there is no one for miles who'll be able to help you."

"We will...I..."

"You don't have a plan, do you? Oh Reverend, I thought you were smarter than that. Has the cancer gotten to your brain?"

"How?"

"I know everything about the people in Olivia's circle. Did you know that I'm the reason you're alive, and not killed the moment you took your first breath? Well, me and Helen." I need to distract him until Buck can get here with the money. "People believed Helen was heartless, but she convinced her father to let you live. Wasn't that nice of her? Both understood it would be better to have a bargaining chip alive, rather than dead. You see, your father came to Helen's father for help. He'd gotten a young girl pregnant; a distant relative of mine. It would have been a scandal if a high-profile government official had a child with someone other than his wife. This man worked for the Hammonds, and any attention drawn to him would not have been good for the family or business. The young girl relished the money they offered her to leave you, and the country, more than her desire to keep you. Helen's father wanted to kill you and your mother. He thought it was the easiest way to clean up the mess. Helen convinced him otherwise."

"Helen asked me to drop you off somewhere to be found. I dropped you off at a monastery five hours away. No paperwork to your name. I didn't learn your mother had registered your birth, after she ran, until I saw you walking through Woodhaven. Those birthmarks in your eyes are rare. I contacted an acquaintance at the registry and learned the boy I dropped off many years ago, and my son lived in the same town. Unaware of their connection."

"I hope you don't expect me to thank you." Reverend John steps forward and his foot breaks through the rotted porch. He loses his balance and tumbles backwards. His foot catches between the broken slats and he can't release it. His gun tumbles down the steps.

Axe over my shoulder, I run for the gun. Wood cracks behind me. Reverend John lunges for my ankle, and pulls me to the ground. The blade of the axe swipes my cheek as it, and I, fall forward.

Reverend John climbs on top of my back. A swift elbow to his side and he's on the ground beside me. I propel myself to my feet, grab the gun, and the axe, and tower over the Reverend. It would be efficient to take his head off here, but I want to enjoy this unexpected present.

"As I was saying, we should talk inside. Up."

Reverend John crawls to his feet and brushes the loose dirt off himself. His eyes calculate, and follow me. "I have two weapons. I don't think it's wise to fight me."

As if on the way to the gallows, Reverend John shuffles along the gravel driveway, head hung low. He stops dead in his tracks when he enters the bedroom. "What the hell is this?"

"Get on the table and you'll live longer. Maybe even see Olivia one last time before you die. Your other option is I kill you where you stand. Up to you."

Reverend John backs up, sits on the table, and then lifts his feet up. I strap him to the table with three straps. One around his legs, one around his torso and one over his head. I crank them as tight as I can. He is not going anywhere.

I place the gun beside my knives, the bottom of the handle aligned with the bottom of the handles of the knives. I run my fingers along the row of weapons. "Which one of these should I use first?" It's rhetorical, and the Reverend knows it.

His eyes are focused on the ceiling. Reverend John changes the subject. "I understand why you hate Olivia, but why would you hurt Calvin like that? Isn't he considered family?"

"Family? I suppose, but he'd never be a true Hammond. He's too skittish and has too much kindness within him. I tried to rid him of that. I failed, and that's when he became a means to an end."

"You are a sadistic monster."

"I'm a lot of things." I look over at my knives. "How about I start with-"
CRASH.

CHAPTER FIFTY

OLIVIA

Charlotte drives along the grass to mask our presence for as long as possible. The only sign of life on this plot of land is John's car and a thin stream of smoke coming out of the chimney of a small faded yellow cabin.

At first, Charlotte and I wanted to drive right through the front of the house. With John's car here and no sign of him outside, we decide against it. We were here to get John, not kill him. We park up the drive and run the rest of the way to the house. Both our shoulders brace for impact against the front door. One. Two. Three.

SMASH.

With both of our bodies colliding with the door, it comes off its hinges and hits the floor. Part of the door frame also crumbles to the ground.

Bullets fly through the wall in front of us and shatter the windows behind. Charlotte and I drop to the ground. She aims at the wall and I push her arm down. "What if John's in there?"

We crawl along the dusty floor towards the back of the house. We hug the corner between the main area and back of the cabin. I peer around the corner. A body is strapped to a metal table. There's an empty metal table alongside it. More bullets dart past us, until clicks are unaccompanied by projectiles.

"Caldwell, you're out of bullets. Why don't you come out here with your hands up and we won't hurt you?" Charlotte announces.

"We won't?" I whisper.

"We need him where we can see him," she whispers back.

"There may not be bullets, but that doesn't mean I'm not ready to fight." A knife whirls past and sticks into the wall above Charlotte's head.

Charlotte nods towards the room. I look forward to filling Caldwell with bullets. Inhale. Exhale. We push to our feet and dash around the corner and into the bedroom.

The top of Caldwell's head is all I can see as he flips the table John is on. It lands on its side and John screams when his arm smashes against the floor. The snap of a bone sends shivers up my spine. John's chest rises and falls in rapid succession.

Caldwell is hidden and in a perfect defensive position. The metal table is for cover, while the other blocks our ability to maneuver to the left side of the room, and the knife station takes up the space on the right of the room. Plus, he has a screen door for an exit if needed. Neither Charlotte nor I can get a shot off. More knives somersault towards us. One catches my arm but doesn't stick. The cut stings and blood trickles inside my sleeve.

A rickety wooden door bounces against its frame. Charlotte crawls on her stomach and unlocks the wheels of the empty table. She pushes it out of the way and it collides with the wall beside me. Charlotte's actions cause no reaction from behind John. Caldwell must have left out the door, rather than using it as a distraction.

"You help John. I'll go after Caldwell." The springs in the door announce her exit.

I scramble for John. "Are you okay?"

Despite being stuck in place, he is out of breath. "I think something's broken, but I could be worse."

"I'm going to release the top and bottom straps. Now the middle one. Ready?" I say.

"Yes." John replies.

"One. Two. And Three." John falls forward and lands in my lap.

Bullets sing outside. I help John sit up. "You stay here. I'm going to find Charlotte."

"I'm not staying here," he says.

"You're hurt," I say.

"I don't care. I'm coming with you," he advises.

"Fine." I grab the largest knife I can find on the floor. "Then take this."

As fast as we run outside, we come to a stop. John almost barrels over me. Charlotte's sprawled out on the ground. Blood oozes through her white suit.

"No!" I scream.

I scan the property and don't see Caldwell. I drop to my knees beside Charlotte. I pat her down but she doesn't have her phone. Shit! It's still in the car's cup holder. I was too focused on getting to John, my phone must be sitting beside hers. "She has a pulse. I need a phone. Our car's parked up the drive and is unlocked. Can you get it? Fast!" I yell.

John runs around to the front of the house. I see one wound and put pressure on it. Charlotte's gun's gone. Caldwell must have it. I still don't see him. John returns out of breath and coughing. His broken arm held against his body. "Here."

"I can't let go of the wound. The code's 2020," I say.

"No signal," John says.

"Fuck!" I say.

"Hang on, I have one bar." John dials and advises an emergency operator what's happened. I'm dismayed when he places the phone on Charlotte's chest, turns on the speaker, and runs towards the barn.

"John, get back here!" I yell.

Charlotte's eyes flutter, and the operator tries to get my attention. "Is someone there? An ambulance is on the way."

"Great, thank you, but I have to go," I say.

"You can't-" the rest of the sentence gets lost in the dirt. I drag Charlotte up against the house. If Caldwell comes back, I need her protected as much as possible.

"Olivia?" Charlotte strains to speak.

"Charlotte! Hang on. Help is coming. Put pressure on your wound. I'll be right back." I run back into the house and grab one of the straps that had secured John to the table.

"I'm going to wrap this around you. Lean forward." It takes many rounds of wrapping to create tension around her slight frame. I crank it as tight as it will go. Charlotte grimaces and sounds like a balloon filling with air.

"Operator?" I ask.

"Oh, thank God. How is she doing?" asks the dispatcher.

"Here, you can talk to her. Charlotte, I have to go find John." I kiss her cheek and put the phone beside her.

A dark blob running in the distance, past the barn, tells me where to start. I push my legs as hard as I can and find both men along the cliff by the edge of the forest. Caldwell and John are a ball of bodies rolling on the ground. There's no sign of Charlotte's gun.

I aim mine, but every time Caldwell gets on top of John, John rolls him back to the ground. Adrenaline is one hell of a painkiller, the way he is fighting with a broken arm. They are exchanging places with each other so fast, I can't get a shot off. They don't register my presence.

The cliff's edge gets closer the more they roll round. They're going to fall over it if they're not careful.

"STOP" I yell. They freeze. John is on top. Both men's faces are red and they heave for air during the break from the fight. "Both of you on your feet." My gun remains focused on Caldwell. John dawdles but climbs off of him. "John, step away."

"Olivia, you don't have to do this," John says.

I avoid his gaze and remain focused on the man who thought he could play puppet master with my life. With my son. I step in front of Caldwell. Close enough to see the whites of his eyes and just out of his reach. Back at Hammond Manor, Caldwell was always stone-faced. Expressionless. Today, his conniving grin is unmasked. His eyes taunt me to pull the trigger. "I have to take care of this. He and the Hammonds have caused my family enough pain. I can't count on anyone else to take care of this. Not the police. Not a judge. I need to do it myself."

"You have enough blood on your hands. Please don't add more. I'm begging you. For me. For Calvin," John says.

213

"Calvin will understand. I'm sorry John." The smooth curve of the trigger welcomes the force of my finger.

Before my gun goes off, John knocks me off balance. I steady myself just as John's shoulder barrels into Caldwell's stomach like a rugby player. They step back and Caldwell teeters on the tip of his toes along the edge of the cliff. I watch in slow motion as he reaches for John's shirt. Caldwell's fingers cling to the bottom edge and he pulls John closer to him.

A scream lodges in my throat and my heart stops. John's going to be pulled over.

Caldwell's foot slips. John's usable arm comes down hard on Caldwell's grasp. Caldwell tilts back over the edge. My legs move at the pace of a turtle as I run towards them. I will not make it. I'm too far.

A trail of screams and a loud thud greet me at the cliff's edge.

CHAPTER FIFTY-ONE

CALVIN

C hlorine and sanitizer tickle my nose. The hairs on the back of my neck stand on edge as my memories bring me back to the prison infirmary. Fluorescent lights radiate off every surface of the waiting room. There is no hiding in this medical center. Down the hall, people sing Happy Birthday. A rare moment of happiness in a place people avoid whenever possible.

It's been two weeks since I was released from prison. DI Whitaker confessed to everything when he found out his father was dead – the manipulation of Officer Cole, and guiding my hand and the knife into Shaylynn while his father held her still, and the tampering of evidence. The Crown prosecutor apologized for everything I'd gone through and looked just as confused at the rest of us. Mom is still furious that the judicial system once again failed. So am I.

Mom sits beside me, her toes tapping in sync with the song on the building's sound system. The dark bags under her eyes carry a weight I'll never understand. Those eyes dance around the room, and travel scenes beyond the one we are in. When her mind wanders, she doesn't go far. I squeeze her hand and bring her back.

"Is it our turn?" she asks, brushing the wrinkles out of her pants.

"Not yet. Soon. You seemed like you were off somewhere. Everything okay?"

"Yes. Yes. Everything's fine. I'd like some water."

Before Mom can stand, a bottle of water is held out in front of her. She takes it and pulls the arm towards her until John's lips are pressed against hers.

"I get that you two are in love, but that's still very weird for me. My Reverend and my Mom."

"We still have some time before our session. Your mom and I can make out so you can get used to it." John wraps the sling-less arm around my mother and sticks his tongue out like he's going to lick her cheek.

"I know you're joking, but please don't."

A pretty receptionist with rose coloured cheeks and bright blue eyes turns to us. "You three can go in now." The red light beside the door goes out and the lock clicks free.

"Is everyone ready to bare their souls to Dr. Sheila? I could really use someone to talk to about being forced to eat Calvin's cooking." John's trying to lighten the mood, knowing it's about to cloud over. He's been doing that a lot at home, too.

"Listen here, you one-armed man. I'll stop feeding you all together, but Mom seems to want you around. So you'll eat what I cook," I say.

"You know, I used to tell you the same thing. Now who's the adult?" Mom takes my and John's hands, kisses them and leads us to Dr. Sheila's door. "Shall we tackle this next mountain together?"

John opens the door and the tea tree oil in Dr. Sheila's diffuser greets us.

Therapy has been hard, but it has helped John and me to see Mom more clearly. The hell she went through as a child and her desire to disassociate from being a Beaumont. How losing her sister and friends affected her. The horrific forced mental and physical conditions she experienced at the hands of the Hammonds. How my minor acts of defiance shattered her heart.

John and I have our own baggage. Losing Shaylynn has been one of the hardest things I've experienced. Some days it's still a struggle to get out of bed knowing I won't see her. I'll carry it, and any other turmoil, if it means I can help Mom find happiness.

CHAPTER FIFTY-TWO

OLIVIA

The air smells sweet from the lilac trees canopying above us. The stone steeple of the church towers overhead, and brings me a sense of peace. I'm where I'm supposed to be in this world. Finally.

The church bell startles a flock of sanderlings when it announces the start of a new hour. Children ignore the chimes and chase each other through the churchyard, while parents caution them to keep their freshly-pressed dresses and suits clean. A group gathers around the barbecue, and wafts of grilling meat and baked potatoes call out to my stomach.

Charlotte stands in the archway of the side door of the church. Her curly blond locks and purple floral dress dance in the soft end-of-the-summer breeze. The beauty of the stained glass windows pales in comparison to her. She's enamored with her conversation with Stan, the son of the owners of the Gosling and Mason pub. Charlotte's so distracted, children run into her while they play, and Stan has to keep her upright. It's nice to see my friend lost in love, rather than work.

John leans over in his chair. "You look beautiful."

"Thank you, but you've said that a hundred times today. It's losing its significance."

"Well, I'm going to keep saying it because it's true."

Charlotte helped me pick out a simple silver dress with an elegant drop neck. It hugs my curves nicely and for the first time in a long time; I feel as beautiful as John says I am. John had the diamond and sapphire necklace I shattered in his office repaired. It sits comfortably around my neck. The blue sapphires match the ties worn by John and Calvin.

Each has a place on either side of me. Their dark suit jackets are strewn over the backs of their chairs. John rolls his sleeves up to his elbows to cool himself off more in the summer heat. He would have preferred to wear a t-shirt with a tuxedo image on it. The shirt would have been much cooler than the polyester one he had on. I almost gave in to his pleas, but Calvin refused to stand beside me if John donned anything but a suit. We came to a compromise, and the t-shirt will come out at the pub for the post-reception party for the adults.

Two years has turned my boy into a man and my heart is full. The remnants of William are gone. All I see is Calvin, a strong-minded, loving human who, with the help of John, has assisted me slay my demons.

Cheers from the crowd draw my attention from the chiseled face of my son. "Kiss her!" yells someone in the crowd. More hollers and whistles follow.

"Well, Mrs. Buckley, should we give the crowd what they want?" John's eyes sparkle brighter than I've ever seen them.

"I suppose we should." John lifts my chin, pulls it towards him, and his soft lips melt into mine.

"Now kiss her like you mean it!" Aunt Maud yells.

John straddles my chair and the crowd cheers.

"You're both insane," Calvin says.

"Insane for each other," John replies.

Calvin and I roll our eyes. John retakes his seat and I pat Calvin's hand. "How about you and I go for a walk before dinner's ready? John can manage the cries for kisses without me."

"I'm sure I can find a nice stand-in. Patty looks pretty good in that yellow dress."

"Seriously, you two are weird." Calvin puts his arm through mine and we break free of the wedding guests. We follow the gravel path to the back of the churchyard. Tilted moss-covered stones line both sides of the walkway.

"I can't believe my little boy leaves for college tomorrow. Couldn't you stay here another day, a year? Forever."

"I love you, but no."

"I had to ask, and I'll continue to ask until I drop you off at the train station."

We stop in front of a shaded, polished stone.

"Two years later, and I still miss her." Calvin's hands hide in his pockets. "Does it get any easier?"

"Not really. I still think about Claire and Whitney every day. It hurts a little less, but it's still there. I'm really proud of you, you know. Many people would have fallen apart after everything you went through."

"It was nothing."

"Give yourself some credit. Therapy is a lot of work and you stuck with it. Most teenagers would brush it off and try to handle the world's problems on their own."

"We did some of it together, and that helped." Calvin brushes some fallen leaves from the top of Shaylynn's gravestone.

"Before I ruin my makeup with tears, let's change where this conversation is going. Not that I don't want to have these conversations. I just want today to be a little less doom and gloom. Have you figured out what you want to do after college? Or are you still thinking of trying a few different classes in your first year and see where it goes?"

"I'm pretty sure I know." Calvin looks at his feet and kicks the clumps of freshly mowed grass.

"Really? And when are you going to fill me in on the secret?" He hasn't been this timid since he was fourteen.

"After the wedding. Or maybe after college graduation."

"So, I won't like your profession of choice?" I take a flower out of my hair and lay it against Shaylynn's stone, under the inscription "A life measured in memories, not years."

"There is a high probability you won't approve."

"Is it illegal?"

"No."

"Then I doubt I'll outright hate it."

"I'm going to get a degree in computer science and criminal justice and apply for MI5."

"Huh. Really?" My heart sinks to my stomach, but quickly rebounds. There are worse jobs he could want. He could turn into a politician.

"See, I knew you wouldn't like it."

"I didn't say that. I want to understand your reason before I decide. You'll be disappointed if you are hoping for car chases and gunfights."

"I want to help those people who don't have anyone else fighting for them. And if I kick a little ass along the way, that's a bonus."

"That is admirable. Are you sure?"

"I've talked to Aunt Charlotte a lot about this. If it wasn't for you and her, I'd still be in prison. She's shared with me the good and bad that comes with the job. So, I know what I'm getting into. I believe it's something I really want to do."

"If that's what you want, I'll support you. Although, I'll have to have a talk with your aunt about keeping secrets from me." I wrap my arm about Calvin's wide frame and we meander back towards the party. "Why didn't you talk to me about it?"

"I figured you'd try to talk me out of it."

"I'll admit, I don't love it. It's dangerous. But so is every other job in this world. Hell, a pile of books could fall on my head at the bookstore and do me in. I'm not naïve enough to think that the world doesn't need people like Aunt Charlotte, or even you, if you go down that road. Just because I left law enforcement, doesn't mean I don't love and respect those who have the courage to join the service and fight the evil in this world."

"You're sure you are okay with this?"

"Yes. But, promise me you won't tell me how many times you get shot at, run over, stabbed, et cetera."

"I promise."

We return to those gathered on the rolling hills of the churchyard. John smiles and waves across the crowd.

"You look happy, Mom."

"I am happy. Agent Lyons."

ACKNOWLEDGMENTS

As I look back on how Olivia Beaumont's journey came to be, where it went, and where it ended, I'm immensely thankful to all the people who helped bring my dream to life.

First and foremost, my amazing husband. His constant encouragement and brainstorming pushed to spend hours, after long days of work, to get the words on the page.

Mom, Dad and Sister have been the cheerleaders that never left my side. I'm sure their friends are tired of hearing about my books!

To Lisa, my editor, and Candice and Megan, my Beta Readers, for your feedback. Without you my stories would have many plot holes and I would use common words or phrases repeatedly, to the annoyance of readers.

Lastly, and most importantly, thank you to you, the readers, for taking time to enter into this world. I hope you enjoyed the journey. I look forward to seeing you on the next one!

ABOUT AUTHOR

N. L. Blandford is passionate about creating awareness around social issues through fictional stories. Her cunning and fearless characters take readers on thrilling journeys rooted in truth. N.L. Blandford donates a portion of the proceeds from *The Perilous Road to Her, The Perilous Road to Freedom,* and *The Perilous Road to Him,* to a charity who supports survivors of human trafficking and/or victims of sexual assault.

N. L. Blandford resides in Calgary, Alberta where she has built a life of dream exploration with her husband, mild mannered dog, Watson, and stubborn but loveable cat, Sebastian. When she is not writing, she works full time as an investigator of fraud at a financial institution.

www.nlblandford.com

nl@nlblandford.com

Instagram.com/nlblandford

bookbub.com/authors/n-l-blandford

Twitter.com/nlblandford

ALSO BY

The Perilous Road To Her

I n book one of The Road Series, *The Perilous Road to Her*, N.L Blandford takes us on a woman's harrowing journey to find her missing sister.

Olivia Beaumont, a Detective in the Toronto Police Service, finds herself dreading calls from her older sister Claire. Olivia's attempts to help Claire fight her drug addiction have only been met with refusals. Ready to walk away, and let Claire hit 'rock bottom', Olivia is drawn back when she learns Claire is missing.

Determined to find Claire, Olivia goes on the hunt for those who have taken her. However, the perpetrators have other plans. Suddenly, Olivia feels the prick of a needle in her neck and her world goes black. When she wakes up she has been transported into the underworld of human trafficking. Greed and sex surround her as she is forced to work for the monsters who have built an empire on the desperate and unlucky.

ALSO BY

The Perilous Road To Freedom

In book two of The Road Series, *The Perilous Road to Freedom*, N.L. Blandford takes us on Olivia Beaumont's harrowing journey to find herself and her freedom.

A survivor of William Hammond's human trafficking ring, Olivia Beaumont longs to forget the past four months. Pregnant, and scared of the ties her past will have to her future, Olivia will need more than denial to battle the monsters of her nightmares, and fate.

Right outside Olivia's apartment door stands a past she thought was dead and gone. A past believed to have been killed with her own two hands. A past that forces her back into a world of power, greed and manipulation.

Will Olivia's stubbornness and determination be enough for her to be able to fight the monsters around her, and those in her head, to retake her freedom?

WANT MORE

Newsletter

Want the inside scoop on what's next from N. L. Blandford and receive exclusive content?

Sign up for the monthly newsletter and to receive the free novella "On The Perilous Road". The story is not available for purchase, is a prequel to The Road Series, and explores the backstory of William Hammond. The character everyone hates to love!

Sign up at https://www.nlblandford.com/

Reviews

I hope you enjoyed Olivia's journey so far. If you liked the book and can spare a few minutes, I would really appreciate a short review on whatever website you purchased the book. Reviews are invaluable to an author as it helps us gain visibility to new readers.

Thank you for reading The Perilous Road to Him. Without you this writing journey would be incomplete.

Manufactured by Amazon.ca
Bolton, ON